MARSH CAT

MARSH
CAT

written and illustrated by
Peter Parnall

Macmillan Publishing Company   New York
Collier Macmillan Canada   Toronto
Maxwell Macmillan International Publishing Group
New York   Oxford   Singapore   Sydney

Macmillan Publishing Company
866 Third Avenue
New York, NY 10022

Collier Macmillan Canada, Inc.
1200 Eglinton Avenue East
Suite 200
Don Mills, Ontario M3C 3N1

First edition
Printed in the United States of America
10 9 8 7 6 5 4 3 2 1

The text of this book is set in 11 pt. Primer.
The illustrations are rendered in pencil.
Book design by Christy Hale

Library of Congress Cataloging-in-Publication Data

Parnall, Peter.
    Marsh cat / by Peter Parnall : illustrations by the author. — 1st ed.
      p.   cm.
    Summary: A huge, wild cat faces new dangers when he moves from his marshland home to a barn during the winter months.
ISBN 0-02-770120-4
    1. Cats—Juvenile fiction. [1. Cats—Fiction.] I. Title.
PZ10.3.P228Mar   1991   [Fic]—dc20   90-25733

for my little girl,
Tracy

Prologue

In the still, brittle air of an early November dawn a crow called out, breaking the vacuum of a freezing night that held the inhabitants of a great dark marsh breathless, waiting for the sun. They couldn't see it come, but Crow could. He was one of the first to see the sky lighten, for he slept high in a dense pine grove growing halfway up a southeast slope, high above Beaver and Mink and Otter. From there he saw it all: Beaver Brook Marsh.

Crow was the first to soak up greedily the weak rays that flickered through his tree. He edged farther from the trunk, toward outer branches that began to whisper as the warming air reached them. Every morning the winds freshened over the marsh, sometimes gently, sometimes with enough force to change the face of the Earth, toppling great trees, uprooting the carefully planned dens of foxes, and sending nests of squirrels crashing to the ground. Sometimes they sent Crow and his friend miles afield without consent. Crow preferred gentle mornings.

From his lightly swaying perch he could see down into

the marsh, still locked in its nighttime armor of cold and quiet. His world was beginning to color as the light increased. The branches around him turned a greenish gray, and before the sun ever struck the dead treetops of the inner marsh, his pine was glowing green.

Far below, beyond the winding beaver dam that created the marsh, stood hundreds of dead hardwood trees, killed by the beaver's flood. From Crow's perch he could see the gray treetops begin to brighten as the sun's fingers searched deeper into the depths of the drowned forest. It turned dark shadows slowly into a sparkling, frost-covered world of hummocks and brittle glassy grasses. Moss and lichens glittered with icy coatings, and the air hole at the top of a beaver house sparkled with large crystals, formed by the breath of the family within.

Deep in the hollow trunk of a giant beech tree an old cat slowly wakened, his subconscious jostled by the snap of a rotten twig too laden with frost to cling to its tree. His whiskers twitched at each new sound as he listened to the surrounding marsh come to life. He listened for the wind, listened to the chortles of a distant crow advising others at a treetop council, and he listened for the pulse of the great Maine woods to quicken as its inhabitants awoke, rose up, and entered their daily worlds. For some, this day would be all the world they would ever know.

Chapter One

Cat, son of a mother as wild as any tiger in Siberia, had been born here in this hollow beech tree many years earlier. Brothers and a sister were born that day, too, but over the years they did not adapt to the rigid rules of nature, and one by one they fell prey to their lack of guile. The extra spark that lets one survive and not another was not in them. Cat's mother had been a barn cat. A smallish, black, skittery barn cat. She had wandered here from somewhere else, looking for a home safe from threats, safe from the cold.

Somewhere during that journey she was struck by a car or perhaps was involved in a one-sided battle, for she arrived at the barn with a damaged eye that eventually deteriorated till she lost its sight.

It was a January night she chose to appear, a numbing twenty-below night that forced the inhabitants of the barn to huddle for warmth and breathe small breaths. There were many cats in residence there . . . some from other places, some born there, some yellow, some black, some gray. When she first crawled hesitantly onto the hayloft floor they stared at her silently.

She made no sound.

For many minutes her muscles were tensed for instant flight, should any make an aggressive move. They didn't. No moves. No sounds. She inched forward, each movement almost unnoticeable, so slow was her progress. Encouraged by the other cats' composure she gradually worked her way among them and shared their warmth, snuggling between two large, long-haired furnaces for the rest of the night. Had she not found this particular barn that very hour, she would not have seen another sun.

All went well for the cat the first few weeks. She ate barn cat food that appeared in orange bowls and now and then a mouse provided a special treat. She seemed to fit into the order of things. Nowhere had she ever done that before. Happy cat. Full cat. Warm cat, basking in the sun on the wooden floor.

One morning she bumped into the edge of the big barn door. Confused, she leaped to the side, away from the hurt, missed her footing on the barn door ramp and crouched, her head assuming an unnatural tilt. Off balance and frightened, now afraid to move, she felt alone again. Her injured eye, blinded now, no longer allowed distances to be truly judged. She could never again make an accurate leap either to hunt or play with a windblown leaf. Slowly she became as clumsy as people and dogs. She withdrew to the safety of being last. Last to eat, last to drink, last to crawl into whatever sleeping nook was left over after the other cats had taken their pick of the warmest and best. Whenever she would try to sneak a tidbit of food before the others were finished she would receive a blow to her blind side, and it sometimes cut deep. Her head tilted more. It did not go unnoticed. She was different.

She was different: She was half-blind, and she was pregnant to boot.

The cat discovered a small hole leading into the darkness of the side of the barn where years before oxen had been stalled and she used this refuge, for none of the other cats could squeeze through the opening to pursue what had now become a tormenting game. It worked for a while. Late at night, after all others had retired to the loft, she would sneak back through the hole and search for a forgotten morsel. A leftover crumb. But now, heavy with kittens, she could no longer fit.

No hole: no food.

The cat was not frightened by memories of life before the barn. Now all she knew was fear of cats, fear of hunger, and an unfamiliar urge to find a den of her very own. It was nothing she learned, that urge to den, for all wild things feel it at the proper time, whether they be robin, mouse, or white arctic bear. Late one night she sneaked through a small gap in the dry laid stone that held up the back wall of the barn, and as soon as her good eye glanced up at the new moon rising, she was as wild a creature as could ever be.

Cat was away again. She picked her way through darkness, past familiar clumps of rhubarb behind the barn, underneath dense thickets of raspberry, traveling downhill slowly, her oversize belly now and then rubbing against a fallen limb when she misjudged its height above the ground.

As she continued down the slope from the barn the soil became more moist, and she placed her feet more carefully. More quietly.

Leopard Frog did not hear her coming. He was intent on filling his belly with mosquitoes. He waited beneath a clump of ferns just where the damp ground turned to marsh, close enough to water to catch the insects when they took flight from their larval stage. Frog had hunted here for many nights. It was his place.

The cat was close enough to smell him now . . . to reach him now. She slowly raised her paw and sighted with her good left eye. Not a whisker moved. Just as the frog flicked out his tongue to trap another mosquito, her paw drove down upon him, all five claws reaching desperately for a meal. She misjudged the distance of course, but one claw caught him in the web of a hind foot as he instinctively leaped toward the water and freedom. She had him! Her other foot shot forward to aid the first, and she had him! She had him! It was her only live catch since she lost her eye, and as she slowly ate she began to relax. She felt somehow whole again. Cat finished her meal, and as the moon continued rising over the distant marsh she began her journey toward it, toward the wildness that dwells in the heart of every cat.

She wound her way through dark spruce woods, skirting the edges of water that crossed her path, searching for a suitable den. An old beech tree with a rotted trunk filled her needs, an old beech tree too close to a beaver's flood to survive. It had grown two hundred years. Then Beaver came, flooding acres of lowland woods, drowning the roots of trees till just poles remained. And skeletons. The beech tree was on higher land than some, just ten feet from the water's edge, but its roots were long. Long enough to reach past the waterline—lucky for the cat. The tree hung on for years after Beaver built his dam, but finally died, became fragile, and during a violent northeast storm the wind did its work. The old tree broke in half, laying bare its center for rot to start. Rot. Because of it Horned Owl had the first home: a nest made in the punky center at the stub's very top. More rot. Raccoon was the next to live high in the old beech tree. His home was deeper down the trunk than Owl's. Woodpecker made several homes over the years, and as water seeped through his holes, the tree decayed further and became more hollow. Finally the rot reached the ground and emerged near a large gnarled root. Mink burrowed there for a year or two. Now the tree belonged to a one-eyed cat.

The days that followed were warm, and hunting was easy. Within a week, four kittens were born inside that tree—four black kittens of ordinary size. Nights were spent safe inside the hollow tree, for Horned Owl, Fisher, Coyote, and Fox hunted hard at night, and they could all make an easy meal of an old, one-eyed cat. In the dim shadows of spruce and ferns the mother cat caught mostly frogs. An occasional snake or unwary mouse was brought home, too, and three of the kittens grew.

One grew more.

The two years that followed were spent in normal cat ways, hunting and sleeping the days away. And surviving, avoiding the dangers that always wait to trap the unaware, the unskilled.

Three of the kittens took after their mother in looks: just black, medium to small, six-pound cats. The fourth grew to an enormous size. Some far-off gene had filtered through from an ancestor long gone: an ancestor living in a wilder age when size and strength were a requirement for life. Unlike the others, he slept by day and prowled the marsh and forest floor at night. He relished a frog that old One-Eye would bring, but he preferred squirrel, hare, grouse, and mouse, and often returned to the den with enough food for all.

His brothers and sister tried hunting at night, hoping to catch something on their own other than frog or snake. A number of times they returned with more succulent prey. One-Eye hunted frogs, by day.

During the following year, their third in the marsh, the three small cats ranged wide, confident in their abilities. One by one they did not return. One by one they met Fisher and Owl.

The old mother cat was quite content to let her huge son do the hunting now, for he returned early each morning with far more than she needed. Far more. And his offerings were tastier than frogs! In spite of the abundance he laid at her feet, One-Eye's condition began to decline, and she became quite thin. Her joints were in pain, and that winter the cold pierced her bones.

From their very first winter the big cat had been the family's main provider of food, for once frogs and snakes entered their cold weather sleep, One-Eye was at a loss. The young cat learned early where hares could hide, and birds roosted in tree limbs too low. He learned to listen. He could sit high up on the hill above the marsh for hours, waiting next to a wild apple tree sprout. Waiting, listening for Mouse to scurry along his shallow snow tunnel intent on a meal of apple bark. The cat waited, listened and learned . . . and grew. At four years of age he was of a size that eliminated all danger from predators smaller than Coyote. Even a lone coyote would have been very foolish to tackle *this* cat!

Late one wintery night, he was laboring through powdery snow after a successful hunt for Hare, dragging the big white rabbit between his front legs, when, without sound or warning, he felt a blow to his back, just behind his shoulder. Instantly a searing pain raced through him, forcing the hare from his mouth and a snarl from his throat. He crouched low over the hare, his ears flattened, and his eyes searched the darkness for the source of his hurt. The spruce trees were black against the dark night sky, and there, there among them was an out of place shape. A fat shape . . . and it moved!

Just as his cat brain registered that fact, Horned Owl launched herself anew. To her, cats meant food, but this time she misjudged size. The owl plummeted silently down toward Cat. When they met, the cat rose up on his hind legs, deftly snared the big bird with his huge front feet and dragged her to the snow. The owl's talons were long enough to strike a lethal blow, but her angle was wrong, and as she frantically tried to bring them to bear the cat bit deep into her chest, breaking breastbone and ribs. She died in an instant.

The hare, forgotten for the moment, lay half-hidden in the reddened snow as Cat plucked mouthfuls of feathers from the owl's breast, now and then shaking his head to rid his face of the sticky feathers and down. He fed on breast of owl. He had no way of knowing it, but he was probably one of very few cats who had ever done that.

When his appetite was satisfied he picked up the hare and plowed home through deep snow. Home to One-Eye and a long, winter night's sleep.

When he arrived, she was gone.

Confused, Cat left the hare in the den and searched around the tree for a sign. At the rear there was an uneven trail through the snow. It wasn't a footprinted trail, but rather a draggy-looking one, a trail that expressed great effort, or distress. A few yards down toward the icebound marsh's edge was a pile of blowdowns: logs that had fallen during stormy days. Foxes denned there before the cats arrived and One-Eye's kittens had tumbled about in the wood-bound caves, playing adult games during warmer days.

The unfamiliar trail led beneath the logs, and there Cat found One-Eye lying on her side, cold and still. He nosed her velvety ear and received no response. For a moment he waited, fully expecting her to rise and follow him home. Nothing. No movement at all.

No longer hungry, and more than confused, he walked slowly up his mother's ragged trail and crawled painfully through the rooty entrance of the old beech tree. Cat ignored the great white prize he had brought for his mother, for now his wound nagged and he was beset with a hollowness in his heart he did not understand. He felt very alone.

Snow began to fall quietly over the marsh, gradually covering all signs of struggle and pursuit, and as it slowly created a clean new world Cat fell into an uneasy sleep.

Chapter Two

On this crisp November morning, as crows discussed their morning plans far in the depths of Beaver Brook Marsh, almost a year had passed since Cat had been on his own, and as he slowly awakened he felt that crispness: a delicate tingle that even deep within his woody den brought the promise of colder days to come. Summer hunting had been easy and on lazy days he had even satisfied himself with meals of frogs. He was never to forget One-Eye and her lessons about Frog. And Snake. Long stalks and battles in the snow were distant in his mind, and a thin layer of fat had snuck beneath his skin.

As he lay upon his bed of decayed wood, trampled soft as peat by years of pressure from the various furry souls that had called it home, Cat heard a bird sound that had puzzled him over the years: a high, faint call that greeted the sun. When the wind was right, when it came from over the hill behind his tree through the dark mass of spruce that extended far beyond his marshland world, he wondered.

Cat certainly knew about birds. He had listened to

Loon many times rolling his eerie whistles across the lake that Beaver Brook nourished and filled. Early in his life, intrigued by the calls and conversations of these big, graceful swimmers, he had paused by the lake's edge and listened. And looked. When Loon called, Cat's hunt for Frog was set aside as he crept through thickets of ferns getting as close as he could to the marshy edge of the lake. If he raised himself tall upon his front legs he could just see over the tops of thick pickerelweed that filled the water along the shore. He saw loons: sometimes one, sometimes three or four. One year he saw two babies, one swimming behind its mother, and the other riding high upon her back. He had seen a baby beaver do that, too. In his travels through the marsh and around the lake he had never come across the loon's nest. Lucky for Loon.

Cat knew of other birds. He knew how tasty was the fat ruffed grouse, he knew about the cleverness of that devil Jay: Jay who delighted in warning all within earshot that Cat was on the prowl. He warned them with scolding shrieks, following the cat till he tired of the game or till Cat chose to crawl beneath a log or a mass of ferns and wait till the pesky bird went about a different chore.

Cat knew Great Blue Heron's gutteral croak and had watched him fish at the edge of pickerelweed, stalking minnows, perch, and baby bass. He knew of woodpeckers who searched the outer layers of his long-dead den tree, drilling holes then searching with their long, sticky tongues for sweet morsels of bug that lived within. Many mornings he had been awakened by the sharp hammering of a woodpecker's bill. He knew of ducks, of geese, and of the fierce gray goshawk who ruled the daylight air, and of course he knew very well old Great Horned Owl.

But this high-pitched crowing from beyond the spruce remained a mystery to cat. It was a positive sound, a dominating sound that expressed no fear and simply stated "I am here! I am here!" Many woods sounds are from creatures who live in fear, tentative creatures for whom quiet and stealth are their only strength, and a strong challenging call is rare from any but the most confident.

He paused when he heard that distant crowing call, and wondered. The life in the marsh was all he knew. He knew it well. This sound drifting in and out on the wind was from beyond his moist, mossy familiar realm. It was a bugle call from away.

The fallen twig that woke him now lay half on the ground, propped up by a mass of golden, dry ferns that grew by the entrance to the den. The sun had been up for some time. The breath crystals at the top of Beaver's house were now gone, melted along with the silvery coatings on plants throughout the marsh. This was a late hour for Cat to be rising, but the easiness of summer had removed his competitive edge, and urgency was not in him. The snugness of the den, the familiar punky smells of the wood that had sheltered him all of his life, and the fact that he had fed heartily the previous evening promoted a contentment more often restricted to his domesticated cousins.

He listened to Crow chortling in the distance, he heard the wind whisper through the upper chambers of his tree stub, and he did *not* hear Red Squirrel or Jay scolding in any way, so all were as content as he. Cat slowly rose to his feet, lifting his bulk one end at a time, and, setting his hind feet in place, moved his front several paces forward till he was stretched out as far as a cat can stretch. His head rose and he arched his back in reverse until every muscle, joint, and sinew was wrung out and in place. Truly a stretch that only a cat can make.

He felt alive now, and became more aware of his wildness as he continued to listen to the sounds of the marsh awakening. When he crawled through the tight entrance to his den he felt the coolness of fall settle upon him.

The entrance to the den was on the northwest side of the tree and a rock large enough for Cat to sit upon lay just to the right, protecting the opening from any harsh north wind. It was covered with moss, and during warmer months he would often lie there for hours, watching the edge of the marsh.

This morning he placed his forepaw on the rock, prepared to do the same before starting his daily rounds, but withdrew the foot quickly, flicking it sharply. The frost that had covered the marsh so completely during the night was now no more than wetness, rendering soggy any plant that could soak it up. With an expression a human might relate to distaste, the huge cat stared at the offending moss a moment. Then, assembling his various dignities, he slowly walked toward the water's edge, obviously less than pleased.

A paper-thin sheet of ice had formed during the night on the surface of the marsh water, but already the sun had begun the melt and Cat was able to quench his thirst with shallow laps from the skim of water on top of the ice. The cold liquid sharpened his focus as it cooled his mouth, his throat, and finally settled in his stomach, bringing attention to the fact that there was an emptiness there.

Cat raised his head, glanced briefly toward the north, through the patches of dried ferns and grasses along the water's edge, then eastward across hummocks and into thickets of the alders that separated the marsh from higher ground where pine and spruce took hold. He chose east, and proceeded walking slowly along the shore, not carelessly, just slowly enough to notice any furtive movement. Movement is the downfall of those who are preyed upon, for often they are camouflaged by cover or color, well hidden until they move, thus betraying their presence, and creating instant risk.

As he moved through the hummocks, Cat found the ice that lay between them too thin to support his weight, but was able to cross by jumping from one to another.

Now, with winter's preliminary advances searching through the land, surfaces were becoming more firm and the hummocks became stable. When he reached the hummock closest to the alders, Cat sat upon it for a moment, watching carefully the rooty alleyways that separated one alder bush from another. Sometimes Frog, feeling safe within the heavy thickets, would leave himself a little too exposed for good health. Then Cat had often been able to begin a successful stalk.

But now cold had driven Frog, Turtle, and Snake to their winter's sleep, so the big cat's efforts were in vain. He slowly stepped into the alders, trying where he could to avoid the shallow waterways that wound among them. Even this huge, marsh-dwelling cat had a distaste for wetting his feet! His path led him to more and more shallow, moving streamlets, and he angled off to the south briefly, to avoid the main flow of them: a flow caused by excess water that trickled over the top of Beaver's dam.

Cat's detour brought him to the westernmost end of the beaver dam. Here it was quite low, as the flooded land beneath it had a very shallow grade, and the dam tapered in height along its two-hundred-yard length from four feet in the center to six inches or so where it ended on the higher ground. It was a very old dam, not resembling the piles of sticks laced with mud one ordinarily thinks of, but more an earthen dike. Over the years repeated applications of mud had provided a firm enough base for grasses, ferns, mosses, and even alders to take root along with water plants. Unless one were quite close, the dam looked no more than an extension of the land, except at the center.

There, a logger had dynamited the dam in an effort to drain that part of the marsh, trying to dry the bottom enough to reclaim the hardwood trees killed by the water. Within a few days Beaver and his mate had filled the eight-foot gap with twigs and branches, packed the spaces solidly with mud and grasses, and within a week their marsh was as deep as before.

Cat walked slowly to the edge of the new construction, glanced about, and lay down. He liked the sound of the water as it trickled over the dam and spilled into a shallow pool four feet below. The leafless, drowned trees on the beaver's side allowed the late fall sun to reach down and warm him as he lay there watching minnows darting about just below the surface. When he was feeling lazy this was a favorite hunting spot.

He had tried often enough when he was younger to trap minnows against the side of the dam with a quick scoop of his paw, to no avail. But earlier in the year, when the dam was lush with foliage, he could lie there well hidden. Waiting—waiting for foolish travelers like

Squirrel, who sometimes used the dam for a bridge! Tired of watching minnows, Cat lay on top of the dam watching beavers adding sticks to their lodge. He didn't understand beavers at all. He had found the dam on a late afternoon's hunt in his younger years when he began to roam. The furry builders were busy repairing their dam that day and showed no fear of Cat as he approached, sat, and watched. He was near the center where they were toiling away, adjusting, prodding, and delivering new packing to hold back the water's flow. At one point a beaver swimming with a small branch in its mouth approached Cat with only its mission in mind, and when it rose from the water to position the stick Cat reached out with a tentative paw. The beaver dropped its load, slid back a bit, and regarded Cat with its tiny eyes. Floating again, it stared, unafraid. The big black shape stood, and the instant Cat reached his feet the beaver's tail hit the water with a resounding smack! He dove out of sight leaving a boiling swirl for Cat to watch, and remember. Many times he had returned to watch Beaver work. He never regarded the beavers as food. He was not a willing swimmer, and they kept to the safety of their watery home when cat was about. It puzzled him to see a furry creature like himself disappear beneath water willingly. Through the years his presence was accepted somewhat, and on warm days he might lie there for hours, watching minnows and beavers. Watching minnows, beavers, and waiting for Squirrel to make an uninhibited dash across the sodden dam.

Filmy layers of cloud slowly softened the warmth of the sun as Cat lay on the dam, contemplating the surrounding hints of cold to come.

As he became aware of the cooling air, Cat slowly rose

to his feet. As he did so the faint whisper of a faraway crowing call reached his ear. He turned his head in the direction of the sound and saw through the naked crooks and spires of maple and oak the dark forbidding wall of spruce that had always protected his marshy world. He heard not another call. There *were* several, but the wind had shifted slightly and sent them south, toward another part of the forest where Deer was searching out the last morsels of hidden green before cold forced his diet to change to harder, more bitter fare: dried, undeveloped buds, twigs, acorns, and evergreen tips of spruce and fir.

The graying of the sky made Cat uneasy. His empty stomach, so far this day christened by only a sip of cold, sent a message as well. He walked slowly along the dam, and at the end stepped off on solid ground. The huge black cat lowered his head and glided, snakelike, beneath and through the brittle lower branches that poked stiffly from the trunks close to the ground: branches that separate the world of spruce from the marsh like so many bars of a cage.

Stopping for a moment, he stood, surveying the forest floor for a sign or a smell. His nose was not keen. His eyes were his guide and, backed up by his ears, they rarely missed a movement or sound. A solitary silhouette of a cat, motionless among the dark woody forms of trees was impossible to see. Unless he moved.

He did not move. Nor did anything else within his view. The ground, covered with needles, fallen twigs, and tiny ferns, seemed bare of life. Not even a red squirrel flicked its tail from the safety of branches overhead. Cat relaxed a bit. There was more land to cover, more time, and in his memory a hunt among these woods was rarely unsuccessful.

He continued on, walking in a more leisurely fashion now. Fifty yards from where he had entered the woods he came upon a large, earthy, scraped patch on the ground, next to a particularly large tree. Cat had seen these before. Some were smaller, but they all had a curious smell. At least to Cat.

Deer had made that scrape, digging through the carpet of needles till he rearranged a square yard of cover, then had relieved himself upon it. He made many of these markers on the edges of his territory, declaring his superiority and his claim to the lands within to all who might be a challenge.

Cat, crouching delicately at the edge of the scrape, sniffed it with some curiosity. He recognized the smell, of course. During his years he had run across these scrapes many times, but was ignorant of their meaning. Nevertheless, before moving on, he gingerly stepped to the center of the disturbance and with none of the traditional catlike preparations, urinated thoroughly. He stepped away from the now reeking scrape of Deer, rather pleased.

Cat's attention returned to the task at hand. The sun had eased higher overhead by this time, and the wind blew gently, removing all traces of moisture left over from the previous night's frost. He continued walking slowly, without any attempts at stealth, glancing about at clumps of drying vegetation as he looked for signs of movement. The woods began to thin a bit along his route: an occasional stump indicating that the area had been logged at one time. Here and there a pine seed had trespassed into the land of spruce, taken hold, and grown into a fine, tall tree.

Farther on the pines became more numerous, and the

ground beneath Cat's feet changed from a fairly solid mat of short, sharp needles and brittle twigs, to a softer footing made from needles of greater length. The clumsiest of animals could walk silently here.

By the middle of the afternoon the air had taken a cooler turn, prompting Cat to travel more swiftly now, though no less quietly than before. He slipped noiselessly around moss-covered stumps, sometimes trotting the length of any blown-down tree that offered him an easier path through heavy brush, or over flooded depressions on the forest floor.

His search for food had taken on a more urgent tone with the coming of grayer skies and cooling air. Gradually circling southward, Cat crossed a logging road choked with tan and gold ferns, and just as he emerged from within the heavy cover he paused, remembering a spring that lay just downhill from where he stood.

The spring never froze, even on the coldest of January days, and hunting had been good there over the years. His pace slowed. A dead larch tree was his goal, for it marked the site of the hidden spring. He well remembered that tall, barkless tree.

During late November of a previous year, during the time Deer is on the prowl seeking a mate, Cat was peacefully taking his ease with a long, sweet drink, planning to lie there awhile before heading back to his beech tree den. He had arranged himself in a comfortable pose, preparing to sleep for a wink or two, when from directly behind him and far too close, a loud snort shattered the tranquil air.

The big cat's nerves became instantly tense, electric almost, and he leaped to his feet to face the threat. Not ten feet away stood a heavily antlered deer, head down, feet planted squarely upon the ground. They stared at each other for an instant or two, then the deer raised his head, quickly stamped each front foot once, and let out another explosive snort. With no more ado he launched himself with a vengeance at Cat. Fortunately, cats are cats. This one was up the dead larch tree before the deer had closed the gap!

Deer circled the tree a time or two, then took a long drink from the spring before returning to his urgent rounds. Cat watched from high in the tree till the deer was out of sight, then lowered himself to the ground. He would always remember that tree. And others.

This day when the tree came into view Cat slowed, becoming more alert, and resumed his slow, hesitant hunting walk. No matter that the ground rose and fell, the big, velvety head stayed on an even plane as he moved silently closer.

A sound!

A quiet rustle.

Cat stopped, frozen. In the silence that followed he could feel the blood pumping through his legs, could hear it in his ears. Then he heard a muffled thump. He knew that sound. It was Hare. Cat crouched, his belly to the ground, and slithered forward like a stream of oil.

Now six feet from the spring and slightly above, he could see the hare through the stems of fern and grass, lapping the cold, clear liquid, unconcerned. The hare's fur had almost changed to winter white, and had just a few telltale signs of summer brown blotching his sides. He was sideways to the view of Cat, and had the hunter tried to make a circling stalk, he surely would have flushed the rabbit too soon. He was too close to change routes now, the only choice was a dash ahead. Surprise and speed had often served him well.

Cat tensed, his concentration preparing muscles for an all-out burst. Then, at the height of all possible tension he leaped forward, his front legs stretched to their utmost, grasping for white fur.

Unbeknownst to Cat, the big hare had just finished his last sip before the attack, and just as the hunter flashed into sight he had raised his head from the surface of the water. Instinctively the hare's powerful hind legs launched him forward, sending him clear across the spring to even more solid footing. Cat landed where hare *had* been. Not gracefully, however, for as the two animals passed by each other, claw had reached fur, with just enough contact to send Cat off balance so he did not land in position for another accurate assault. He turned quickly. As he did so, Hare was just disappearing under a log on the other side of the spring.

Cat followed desperately, but the rabbit continued beneath another, lower log, too small a space for his pursuer to negotiate. The cat scrambled over that one, losing his grip on a thick pad of moss growing on top. He jumped to another and listened, as the fortunate hare scuttled through a maze of fallen logs and twisted branches.

Maybe when he was younger he might have been agile enough to pursue Hare through this tangle, but not now. By the time he searched through it all and found the rabbit's last trail it would only have led to an impenetrable lair.

Frustrated, hungry, and ill-tempered, Cat returned to the spring and filled his very empty stomach with sweet

water. He then followed the spring's gentle flow as it wound through a small bog. Beyond the bog it became a streamlet and curved southeastward, flowing down a gentle slope toward the marsh. Cat followed it, hoping to find some foolish creature attracted to a drink, some creature not so agile as Hare.

When the moving water reached a point between two large hemlock trees, the land beneath it dropped sharply downward, creating a miniature waterfall. Bare rocks bulged from beneath clusters of heavy, gnarled roots, indicating the springtime flow was a greater force. Below the trickling fall the water had cut deep, forming steep, rocky walls—walls high enough to hide Cat, or even Deer, from any unfriendly eyes. The hemlocks grew thick along each bank, and in some places they leaned over the stream, forming a tunnel. Many times Deer had traveled here, sometimes by choice, cooling himself on a hot summer's day. Other times, when pursued by coyotes or hunters, he used the cover of boulders and trees as an escape route to safety within the depths of the marsh.

Cat picked his way carefully around large rocks, searching the spaces between for a possible meal— maybe a tardy frog? But frogs and dry rustling leaves are not a match. He continued, working his way down the steep streambed slowly.

Fifty yards downhill from the little waterfall the slope became less steep, the exposed rocks smaller, and the growth of hemlock thinned along the rim of the stream's bank. From there Cat could see through the woods, and his gaze followed the water's course to the point where it widened, slowed, and joined the waters of the marsh. He again drank deeply, easing the ache that hunger fueled within him. As he raised his head a single snowflake drifted past his nose and came to rest upon a jet black paw.

Just as he looked at the flake, Cat heard a sharp, unfamiliar sound. A metallic sound, a clink, of sorts, not unlike the tinkle of an ice shard falling from a limb. He knew all the sounds that belonged in the marsh: the wind sounds, the creak and groan of rubbing limbs, the snap of a twig. He knew that the wind in November played different tunes than it did in June. He knew the sounds of the strong and those of the weak with whom he shared this marsh of his. Those sounds could either comfort him or demand attention, letting him sleep or prowl . . . or hide.

But this struck a different note. He had never really known a sharp stab of fear. Nor did he now. Caution, caution, and a sliver of anxiety that made his heart skip once led him to creep up the side of the rocky bank and peer over the edge into the adjacent woods. Snow fell gently now as Cat searched slowly for any shape out of place, and he listened for sounds that did not belong. All was quiet. All was in order.

Abandoning any hope of success by the stream he climbed atop its bank and proceeded slowly down the slope, toward the marsh.

The scolding of a distant squirrel made him turn his head.

Something amiss.

Just as he began to turn and face the chattering sound, a rock by his foot exploded into dust! An instant thereafter an ear-shattering *crack!* split the air.

Cat froze, unable to determine the source of the sound. His heart raced, and he began to feel pain where a sliver of stone had creased his leg. His glowing eyes searched the hill beyond, covering every stump, every tree . . . but not quite.

Not quite *all* of every tree.

Twenty feet up in a big oak tree crotch perched a two-legged thing, holding a long, black stick. Cat's gaze shifted there when he sensed a move, and just as he did the stick belched fire, startling the cat into a sideways flinch. To his right the ground erupted, spraying soil and pebbles, and again the air was split by the lightning sound.

This time Cat reacted. In a desperate dash he covered ground to the safety of the streambed wall, leaped down, and, hidden under a mass of hemlock roots, he gasped for breath. Hunger was now all but forgotten.

The cat, used to being dominant, used to familiar dangers, now felt fear. An Unknown had assaulted him in his domain, and brought him pain.

The snow fell harder as light faded beyond the creek bed walls. Within the protective cave of roots Cat licked clean his minor wound, and with his teeth tweezed free an offending piece of shrapnel rock. Fine snow continued falling, the tiny flakes spaced closer now, the kind of snow that does not give up.

When darkness obscured the streambed rocks Cat emerged from his cave. He was now just another black, Maine woods shape, heading home. He stayed in the cover of hemlock as he followed the edge of the marsh, traveling north. It was darker there. His blackness wouldn't betray him against the snow. The thickening white blanket was up to his belly now, but it was a fine, light snow, and offered no resistance as Cat plowed through the darkness.

All others sat tight in their roosts and lairs, waiting for light to reveal ghosts and marshmallows.

Finally his beech tree loomed out of the night. The tired cat thrust his head down through the snow, his body followed, carving a tunnel to the entrance of his lifetime home. He lay down slowly, and after a lick or three to his wounded leg, fell into a restless sleep, still hungry.

From the shelter of his hole higher up in the beech stub, Screech Owl watched as snow fell silently through the darkness.

Chapter Three

Cat woke many times during the night: sometimes driven awake by memories of exploding rocks, his heart briefly racing as he recalled images of bursting light erupting from trees. Sometimes his wound urged him awake, prompting care, and reminding him of things he did not understand. Hunger was there, too, a constant needle that made contentment impossible, and security a near-forgotten shadow in his mind.

The only sound that reached him deep within the den was the faint, questioning call of a distant crow. Crow, intimidated by the new world born this day, called for the support of his friends. Those creatures not born to solitude became ill at ease when snow erased the details and accents of the forest floor. They felt more alone, more vulnerable.

Cat pushed his great wide head through the snow that had drifted over his entrance during the night and stood, half-exposed, listening. Crow had been joined by a friend or two, their animated chortles indicating the pleasures of compatible company.

Cat pricked his ears. From far to the northwest, through the spruce woods drifted the strange, challenging call he had wondered about so many times. Some years it had a higher, more strained ring to it, but the language was always basically the same: "Morning and I have arrived hand in hand, and it is good!" Whether the weather was sweet or foul the message was always the same.

He pushed out of the opening and plowed through the still powdery snow to the marsh shore. Cat pawed aside the snow and as his foot pressed against the still paper-thin ice, it cracked, letting water seep up over its surface—enough for a full, deep drink.

His hunger temporarily eased, he turned his gaze back up the rise and beyond the den. There would be no easy hunt this day. Definitely no frogs, snakes, or juicy bugs, and Squirrel would lay low most of the day through, contemplating the new hazards this white stuff had presented. His rich, red-brown fur did not blend in well with snow. Most of his winter stores were buried over a large area of ground, but some was right in his tree. Tucked away for just such days as this.

Cat walked deliberately northwest, up the rise and through the fringe of spruce. Boughs were laden with coatings of snow, forming caves and tunnels that hid his progress from above. Now and then he brushed too roughly a heavily laden branch, and it dumped its load upon him. Blackness emerged with a quivering shake and a flick of tail. One more shake and barely a flake kept its hold on the rich, glossy coat.

He approached a lumpy ridge that wound beneath the snow: a stone wall that once held in the cows when this dense woods had been a field. He felt carefully for solid footing, and crossed over the wall. The other side had been protected by the drift of the wind and the snow was not so deep along that side, so Cat followed the wall for over a quarter mile, poking his nose or a paw into the occasional gap that snow had not filled. He probably passed a hundred mice who had nests deep within that wall.

At one point the narrow trail of an earlier traveler crossed his path and entered one of those dark gaps.

Cat pressed his face to the hole and took a deep whiff . . . ugh! The musky smell of Weasel lingered there. Weasel, now dressed in his winter whites, was patrolling the inner recesses of the old stone wall, with a mouse in mind.

Abandoning the cover of the stone wall, Cat followed the stream southwest, farther than he had ever been before. The character of the trees he passed changed from the dark, familiar spruce and thick, close-growing pine to a more open woods, filled with very large pine. The even spaces between the huge trees were filled with seedlings, their tops barely showing above the snow. They were green polka dots . . . marching. The order of them made Cat uneasy.

He scanned the canopy of trees overhead and broke into a snow-scattering lope that took him across the offending grid of baby trees to the opposite side of these man-made woods where a lone spruce stood, offering cover again under low-hanging boughs. The cat crouched there a moment, looking back at his trail while he caught his breath.

He then turned and slithered beneath the limbs on the other side of the tree. Before him spread an expanse of white birch trees, extending as far as he could see.

He regarded the sight for some moments. There was something ominous about these woods. There were no shadows to guard his anonymous nature, no rocks or ravines to hide him from view. It was a bright, rather cheery piece of land, surely no place for a black marsh cat to be.

He lay beneath the spruce, content to put off any decision to move on, as he examined the white on white expanse laid out before him.

Then, a movement!

A small black spot moved. Cat tensed, and his whole being concentrated on that one small spot. A few seconds passed, and it moved again! Now he recognized it as the dark-rimmed tip of a long white ear. Hare!

This one had its white winter coat. Not a speck of brown remained. With furred lid drawn across its liquid dark eyes and ears laid upon its back, this rabbit became part of the snowscape beneath the birches—until it made that vulnerable move.

Cat waited, unsure of the best approach. He had no chance of a successful stalk out there in the naked white of the sparse birch growth. Nothing there to hide the blackness of him. So he waited, well hidden beneath this dark, snow-covered arm of spruce.

The hare moved a pace forward and paused to nibble on some small treat left exposed above the snow. As it chewed, the dark tips of its ears twitched almost imperceptibly, but to Cat they were flags, flaunting, inviting him to dine. Hare began to circle in his slow, hesitant search for morsels, sometimes disappearing in a slight dip in the snow, sometimes appearing totally exposed. His path wound closer, and the tense cat waited. He knew he was no match for Hare in terms of speed, especially in the snow. These big white rabbits were also called snowshoe hares for good reason: their oversize hind feet were thickly clothed in fur, permitting them to move about the snow without sinking in too far. Numerous times they had saved Hare's life. Hare browsed closer, unaware of the golden eyes fixed upon him, and Cat waited.

Suddenly, from above his line of sight, Goshawk hurtled into view, her feet thrust forward. Hare was aware of the danger too late, and in midleap he was struck hard enough to be tumbled upon his side. He kicked fiercely at the hawk with powerful hind legs but the bird dodged the stroke with a pump of wings and affixed six of her eight talons deep within the body of the struggling hare. In a moment nought but still white fur lay beneath the victorious bird.

Goshawk adjusted herself upon her prize, and mantled the form with widespread wings, as if protecting it from prying eyes. She then plucked beakfuls of fur, laying bare a patch of skin, and began to dine. The hawk was unaware of a fierce, unwavering gaze from beneath the nearby spruce.

Cat gathered himself, hesitated for a moment as his senses and muscles reached a compatible peak, then launched toward the pair in the snow. The hawk lurched backward in surprise as the big cat closed with a half-dozen, snow-flinging bounds. She prepared to defend her catch by first lowering her head and spreading her wings, doubling her apparent size. But Cat was too big. He was not impressed. Had she stayed to fight, it would have been her last.

The disgruntled bird took to the air, circled once over-head, then flew off to another hunt. Cat turned his attention to the stolen prize.

When he had eaten his fill—gorged, in fact—Cat stood up. His gaze searched through and beyond the boundaries of birch, where here and there shadows hinted of different growth. Off to the left an uneven, dark shape peeked from behind the vertical bars of birch—a very large, dark shape. It warranted investigation, for the cat was tired, and large, dark shapes held promises of shelter. He picked up what remained of the hare and slowly slogged off through the snow.

The thing turned out to be a massive rock. On the near side grew birch, and on the far, spruces and hemlocks. On top of the rock a stunted, somewhat frayed wild apple tree poked its branches above the snow, and beside it lay a large hollow log. The log was covered, too, but one end was slightly exposed.

The sides of the rock were steep enough so as to be free of snow, and Cat examined carefully the cracks and crevices for possible shelter. The rock was really a mammoth outcropping of exposed ledge. It emerged from beneath the ground on the slope of a gentle hill, and to the left of where he stood the cat saw an easy approach to the top. He decided to investigate the log.

It was indeed hollow, and very large. Cat dropped the remains of Hare at the entrance, thrust his head inside, and sniffed a number of times. He smelled the faint odor of raccoon, but not enough to believe one lived there now. He crawled carefully inside.

The soft layers of rotten wood reminded him of his beech-wood den, and the memory comforted him. He managed to turn around a couple of times, though it was a tight squeeze, and lie down, his head facing the opening.

The afternoon light dimmed, and though he could have easily slept, Cat lay awake, very aware he was far from home. There were other odors within this log besides Raccoon's, though hers was the most dominant by far. He could smell Mouse, just a tad, and Skunk. What intrigued him most was that he also detected some cat. His nose was certainly not sophisticated, but he *did* recognize cat. The air was very still outside the log. Inside, Cat felt warm, snug, and not a little drowsy as he began to digest the long-awaited meal.

Then, louder than he had ever heard it before: the raucous, challenging call that had puzzled him for years rang out! *"Errr-er-er-er-eeeerrrrrrrr!"*

It seemed to leap at him from the other side of the birch woods. The sound was repeated three or four times, then was silent.

Sleep for Cat seemed a distant thing, but gradually the darkness, the comfort of his shelter and the familiar odor of cat eased his nerves, and the big cat slept. During the night warmer air filtered through the woods, and the powder snow settled, forming a firmer base. A horned owl paused in a tree at the edge of the birch grove hoping to spy a meal making its way across open ground. It saw the signs of Goshawk's struggle with Hare: tufts of fur and trampled snow, and the trail of Cat leading off through the trees. Seeing no movement on the ground below, the owl flew silently off toward a more productive stand. *"Eerr-er-er-er-eeeerrrrrrrrrr!"*

Cat was jolted from his sleep. The call was repeated, again and again. His ears pricked to attention! His eyes adjusted to the glare of sun on snow as he slowly edged toward the entrance of the log. He was not hungry, but naturally was lured to the meat he had left outside the night before.

It was morning. Late morning, in fact. The sun was high, and the snowy woods sparkled from the light of it. As he crawled into the light, Cat's heart did a double thump.

There, crouched on the opposite side of the rabbit carcass, and facing him squarely, was a small gray cat! Their eyes locked.

The newcomer froze, terrified by the sight of the huge black shape. She had left the barn on the farm nearby early that morning for no other reason than it was a bright, sunny day, and she felt like it.

The other cats with whom she shared the hayloft nooks and crannies were slug-a-beds. They hunted most of the night in the bowels of the barn for mice and rats, and tended to while away the day lounging about, making sure they expended no more energy than necessary. She, on the other hand, was a day-cat, and took advantage of the dry food doled out by the human who fed the horses. She didn't like it much, but it was free, and she didn't have to work for it.

Rooster liked it, too. He seemed to think the cat food was for him, and would often drive them away from their bowls and take what he pleased. If they objected, he flew at them, pecking and hammering with his feet till they retreated. Several times a day, if Rooster was out of sight, she jumped upon the tall, wooden box where two orange bowls held the dried kibble bits. Now and then she discovered a treat, left over from human food of the night before.

This morning she had been encouraged by the brightness of the day to venture farther from the barn than she normally did. The powdery snow of the day before had settled some, making footing more sure, and she was light enough so that, here and there, she could even walk on top without breaking through. The cat had no particular mission in mind, just a stroll. Ordinarily she never went farther than the entrance to a logging trail that began beyond the orchard on the other side of the house.

The shadows of the woods were a mystery to her. She knew danger was there, somehow. Many of the barn cats had gone to hunt there, and some had never come home. The only *old* cats in the barn were not woods prowlers.

This morning the sun lit up field, orchard, and woods alike. Snow reflected light into the shadowy places, and they seemed safe. The little barn cat walked slowly to the entrance of the log road, and turned down it. A few yards farther on she turned right, along a path that led to a large patch of young birch woods, and as she passed a stack of freshly cut logs, a sassy red squirrel chattered. He sat, twitching his tail, just letting everyone know an uninvited cat was on a stroll. In a moment, Bluejay arrived, joining in on the scold. He followed for a while, then tired of it, flying off to other adventures.

The little cat found the birch woods to be a cheery place. She had never been this far before, and ordinarily that alone would have made her nervous. But there seemed no possibility of dangers here. Too bright. Just too bright and cheery. She went a few yards into the birches. Looking to her left, she noticed some yards farther on there was a disturbance in the snow, and walked over to see what it was. Bits of fur lay about, the surface of the snow was greatly mussed, and here and there she saw pink stains. She was intrigued by the smell of meat, though she didn't know what kind it was. She followed the trail as it wound through the woods, all the way to the top of a very large rock.

She found the carcass of Hare in the snow, hard by the entrance to a hollow log. How lucky she was! A free meal of meat. Better than that dried stuff back at the barn. She began to feed.

At the sight of the monstrous black shape that emerged from the log, the little barn cat stiffened in absolute terror. She knew this was a cat, for he *smelled* like a cat! He looked like a cat. But he was three to four times the size of any cat she had ever seen. During her life she had known only small six-or-seven-pound, in-bred, not really too healthy, barn cats. The one in front of her was a whole different thing!

They stared at each other. Neither cat moved their eyes, their whiskers, or even a hair. Cat had not seen another of his kind since One-Eye's death. Indeed, he had only a faint recollection of his siblings *or* his mother. This creature in front of him stirred no feeling of pos-sessiveness over the carcass nor aggression of any sort. He was simply fascinated that she existed. Neither cat uttered a sound.

A moment passed, probably a lifetime to the smaller of the two, then Cat very slowly, deliberately, lowered him-self to a lying position, and just as slowly, blinked his eyes. The barn cat tensed when Cat moved, but when he blinked she visibly relaxed, and she, too, lay down. They remained like this for some moments, alternately staring at each other and at the meat lying between them. The big cat then stretched his head forward and lifted a tiny piece of loose meat from the carcass and chewed it

slowly. The barn cat, now reasonably certain *she* was not to be eaten, did the same.

When each had consumed what was probably no more than a ceremonial portion, they washed their paws with great enjoyment and thoroughness. There was a certain amount of ceremony in that as well. So, they were of the same tribe after all . . . of that the little barn cat was convinced, and it was obvious that Cat enjoyed her company.

The sun was at its full height for a November day, so to escape the harshness of the snow-reflected light, Cat rose, and slowly entered the comforting dusk within the log. After a moment of indecision, the little barn cat followed.

Crow and a friend had been sitting at the top of a pine tree overlooking the rock as the cats fed, washed, and disappeared into the depths of the log.

They were adept at finding leftovers. When they were satisfied the two were safely tucked away, the birds glided down to the rock, landing several yards from the sparsely covered bones. They listened, their heads cocked to the side, then, satisfied with the stillness within the log, proceeded to the carcass and stripped the remaining morsels from its bones.

The two within the log slept for several hours. Cat awoke twice. The first time he was a bit startled by the unaccustomed warmth of the little body lying against him. The second time he felt an internal warmth and security that preordained his soundest sleep in months.

Chapter Four

The little barn cat woke first. It was late afternoon, and the birch woods were already turning blue-gray. The sun had dropped behind the feathery horizon of evergreens growing to the west of the birches, and thin clouds overhead reflected shades of pink. The colors darkened to pinky reds as the sun sank farther toward other worlds.

She was restless, and the sense of it raised Cat from his sleep. He saw her in the entrance of the log: a small, dark shape, silhouetted against the graying birch trees.

She looked back at him, then walked out upon the snow. It was colder now, and the daytime melt had crusted over, making it easier for her to move about. She sniffed at what Crow had left behind. Nothing left to satisfy more than a mouse. They *like* bones! She returned to the entrance several times, as if beckoning Cat to follow. He was reluctant to leave this rather snug log. He wasn't hungry enough to set out on a hunt, and night was fast approaching. Rather a pleasant time to take good advantage of a comfortable, safe den site.

She would not return inside, and though Cat certainly

could not reason, her actions did make him uncomfortable. Each time she headed away from him he felt something, and he didn't like it. When she turned to face him he felt better. More calm, somehow. The last time she headed away, she climbed several yards down and away from the rock. Cat was uneasy when the female disappeared from his sight.

He crawled out of the log and from that vantage point atop the rock, saw the little form walking back down the path they had traveled earlier. She stopped, turned, and stood looking up at the big shape on the rock. She took two small steps back in his direction, and as she did so, Cat stepped gently down the trail toward her.

The two walked easily through the birch woods, abandoning the ragged trail of the day before for the smooth crust that had formed on the surface of the snow.

Horned Owl had returned to try his luck in the open woods, and perched in a pine, watching the two cats make their way across the ground. If the smaller one had been alone Owl surely would have had an easy meal, for he had dined on cats many times. The Marsh Cat—well, that was quite another story. Once before a horned owl had learned that the hard way.

The two passed the pile of logs where Squirrel had chattered, and turned down the logging trail toward the entrance to the orchard. As they approached what was obviously more open space than Cat had ever seen, the more nervous he became. His companion continued right out of the woods into the orchard without hesitation.

Cat could see only danger there; no places to hide! There were a few old apple trees scattered about, but whoever traversed that space was vulnerable. Vulnerable is something woods dwellers cannot afford to be.

His instinct for stealth would not let Cat walk out into the open, and when the barn cat sensed he was no longer at her heels she turned. She did not understand why he hesitated, and called to him softly. He did not move. She walked back to where he stood, by the edge of the woods, turned and walked slowly away from him. He did not move this time, either. Again she returned, puzzled. This land was familiar to the little cat; she felt no dangers here, and though she had no capacity to know Cat's reason for holding back, she knew he was uneasy.

Cat was a watcher. Watchers do not put themselves in positions where *they* can be watched. Just not natural. Not safe. There was no way he would allow himself a disadvantage.

She sensed his desire to stay close to cover, so when she again began walking away, she moved along the edge of the orchard close to the woods. There was about five feet of low growth and small pine between the open space and a stone wall that paralleled the border of the open space, and Cat chose to travel there. He failed to understand why his friend did not do the same.

They walked a short distance through the snow, the female in the open, Cat walking by her side, but hidden within the screen of baby pines, and again the big cat stopped. He stood, transfixed, staring up the hill at a rectangle of light. From behind it drifted the sounds of music and an occasional voice.

Cat had no experience with such things. The clarity of day and glimpses of the moon were the only light he had ever known, and this square light that made noises was a puzzle indeed. His companion was not in the least intimidated by it, for she had passed by the window at night hundreds of times on her forays into the orchard and beyond. He sensed her confidence, nevertheless, he chose to climb over the stone wall and continue along the other side. They walked on, separated by the snow-covered wall, till the sounds that made Cat uneasy receded into the night. Then the wall ended. Or rather, took a right-angle turn to the left. At this point, Cat jumped upon the wall, saw that the female was following it still, and rejoined her as she wound around snow-covered stumps, clumps of maple shoots, and an occasional fallen stone.

The wall led directly to a higher, more tightly fitted mass of stone: the foundation of an ancient barn. In that wall of rock there was a gap, through which many cats had ventured over the years. It was their private gateway to hunts, to private strolls, to whatever adventure they wished to pursue unnoticed. It had been old One-Eye's last contact with meanness and discomfort. To Cat it seemed she had led him to a rocky den. The barn cat walked through without breaking her pace, but when he followed, the only part of him that entered easily was his massive head. The rest squeezed through on his belly, barely.

This was not a den at all! Just a crawl space beneath the barn. It had housed pigs and chickens in years past, but now held only piles of old wood, rolls of used chicken wire, and various items that should have been dumped, but were saved, in hopes their use again would save a dollar or two.

The female walked directly to a large, vertical beam

that rose from the floor and went up through a hole in the floor overhead. She looked back at him, then proceeded to climb it, and went out of sight through the hole. He did the same. Well, almost. He climbed the beam, but upon reaching the hole found that not even his head would fit through. He backed down to the dirt floor. The female returned and repeated her climb, then stuck her head through the hole, puzzled that he had not followed her. After a moment she climbed down again, sat near him, and washed her right forepaw.

Cat was somewhat uneasy here . . . there was a lot of unfamiliar space around him, and he did not like it. The only thing that kept him from returning to the woods was the fact that the little cat seemed so at ease here. In a few moments he became bored watching her tend to her paw, got to his feet and walked through a slot left by a missing board in a wooden partition. The wall had sealed the pigs and chickens in this end of the barn. The back.

The ground slanted sharply upward on the other side of the wall to a point where Cat found he could barely move about. He could walk easily between the massive beams that supported the upper floor, but could not squeeze under them from one space to another. Between two sets of beams, where they joined the foundation wall, he found layers of old hay. It had fallen there when the floor was replaced below the hayloft on the second floor. Toward the front corner of the barn he came to a most disagreeable piece of ground. Smelly. Ugh! He was crouching just below a horse stall. Years of urine had leaked through the floorboards overhead, saturating the ground beneath. The cat turned from that place. He returned to the different alley of beams where he had discovered hay, and there found his little guide snugly curled, already asleep.

When Cat approached her she raised her lids halfway, uttering a small, contented cat sound. This seemed a safe enough place. He lay down carefully beside her and closed his eyes. The barn cat had slept there many times.

The following morning: a familiar sound rang out. . . ."*Eeerr-er-eer-er-eeeeeerrrrrr!*"

Cat awoke totally alert. The sound that had caught his attention for years was now directly over his head! His eyes widened as he strained to hear other sounds coming from above. There were none.

The sun had not come up yet, but it would not have mattered, as the creatures of the barn were not regulated by the rise and fall of the sun, but rather, by the appearance of Man. When he opened wide the huge, white barn doors twice a day sunlight flooded the nooks and crannies within, and food appeared shortly thereafter.

Food. Food was the pendulum that governed the pulse of this barn: hay and grain for horses and sheep, corn and meal for chickens, leftover everything for mice and rats. And cats? Why, that awful dry stuff One-Eye had disliked so much, of course.

Barn cat woke, rousing herself slowly. She knew there was no need for haste, here in the barn. She again carefully washed her paws with slow, deliberate strokes of her raspy tongue. When they were done to her satisfaction she began on her side, just below the shoulder. Progressing past her thigh, she then stretched her hind leg to its fullest extent and with her tiny front teeth, incised free from her skin a tiny mat of hair near her tail. Cat watched her with great admiration. Having completed her toilet, the little cat rose and walked leisurely the length of their beamed den. Cat drew confidence from her easy bearing here in this foreign place.

Surely no dangers lay here, for one so delicate could never survive anything but the most pleasant conditions. He followed.

Halfway up the grade beneath the barn was a man-made opening in the foundation two feet square. The two cats filed out through it and climbed over a large stone platform: the step from which cows used to enter the barn. They followed the foundation wall closely, then turned the corner at the front of the barn. In a warmer season Cat might have been alarmed at the sight of trucks and cars parked along the fence close by, but some snow remained, softening the shape and colors of man-made things.

He *was* startled by a sudden flood of light as he turned the corner. The sun never made such abrupt changes! A large light was mounted above the central barn doors, and it illuminated a quarter acre of the area in front of the barn. Cat hesitated a moment, again contemplating the dangers of exposed movement. Then he followed.

The two reached the center of the great barn doors, where Man always left a five-inch space, unless a north-west rain drove hard, so cats and chickens could come and go without restraint. Should a sheep or horse get loose within the barn, the opening was too small for escape.

Barn cat entered first, and Cat followed willingly. He felt much more at home with the darkness and smells that confronted him here.

Straight down the center aisle they went, halfway the length of the barn, before coming abreast of a large wooden box with a slanting top. She jumped easily to the top of the box. Cat waited on the floor, at least till he heard her chewing on something crunchy! Images of tasty grouse bones came to mind, the ones he used to relish cracking open so he could reach the rich marrow. He jumped up beside her and looked inside the large orange dish. There were little star-shaped things in it that Barn cat was eating with gusto.

Whereas the small cat could pick up just two at a time, Cat could fit a half dozen in his mouth at once. And he did. He did not like them. The bits had the consistency of cedar bark dipped in sand, but there lingered about them the faint odor of fish, and that pleased him.

Earlier in the fall, he had been wandering alongside Beaver Brook, not hunting, but nevertheless keeping an eye out for any opportunity that might present itself, when he happened by a small pool. The level of the brook had dropped drastically by the time maple leaves had begun to turn, forming a series of landlocked pools. Most were empty or contained only a resident frog.

Hunting had been good the previous day, he had eaten well, so Frog did not tempt him. But *this* small pool contained a small sucker. The fish had been far upstream as the brook's waters began to diminish, and by the time he had realized the dangers of this driest of seasons, he could make his way only partway to the beaver's marsh before he was securely trapped by a gravel bar. The fish had been there for several days, unable to feed, and lay in a weakened state when Cat happened by. Only three or four inches of water covered him, and Cat had but to reach out for a meal. He liked fish. A rare treat.

Though these hard little kibbles were a sorry substitute for streamside Sucker, Cat ate his fill.

Barn cat finished before he did, and sat on the box cleaning the sides of her face and muzzle with thoroughly moistened paws. When the big cat turned to her she walked from the box to a five-foot high section of oak log standing alongside it. From there she jumped down to the third step of the hayloft stairs and trotted up to the second floor. Cat followed. Except that *he* jumped to the sixth step, with little effort.

They crossed the landing from the right side of the barn to the left. By this time Cat trusted the lead of the little cat and followed her with little or no question. Had not everything gone well since they met? He could not put it that way, but in his heart was a feeling of warm confidence.

Together they climbed eight tiers of irregularly stacked hay bales. This time Cat was in the lead, for he could leap up three to her one. When she reached the top she led him over to the back corner of the loft where there was a large space between two bales and another had been placed on top, forming a small cave.

She hopped gently into the space, and Cat followed. There he found a padding of loose hay that had been oozled and snuggled into a soft, shallow dish. The big, wild cat lay down facing the opening, as is the habit of wild things, his length stretching three-quarters the length of the bale. Barn cat curled beside him in a more domestic pose, warming herself against his ample belly. As fingers of light began to poke through gaps in the barn's ragged rear wall, they slept.

Chapter Five

"Eeerr-eer—er-er-eerrrrrrr!"

The call rang through the barn, bouncing from beam to wall, searching out the inhabitants of every hidden lair.

"Eeerr-eer—er-er-eerrrrrrr!"

The sound was as crisp and clean as sun and air. It announced boldly that the world of a fresh new day had arrived, and that it was good.

Mouse heard it clearly. He would rather not have, for he and his hundreds of kin were now snuggled deep within hidden nests throughout the barn, and many were resting after spending a long, dangerous night foraging for food.

Cat was startled awake by the sound, and the nearness of it. The volume! At first he was uneasy with the unfamiliar surrounding, but the composure of the little cat lying next to him was comforting. The raucous call was nothing more to her than another barn sound that blended in with the rustling of sheep and the occasional clunk of a horse hoof against the wooden floor.

"Eeer-er-er-er-errrrrrrrrrrrrrrrrr."

This time the call ended with a long, drawn-out lowering of tone, a less demanding note, indicating the perpetrator had accomplished his task and was now readying to set about pursuing interests of his own.

Cat raised his head above the level of the hay bale that lay in front of him. From there all he could see were more bales stacked to the ceiling, so he slowly climbed over that bale, and in his most cautious crouch crept forward to the edge of the green precipice.

Below him, standing beside one of the orange bowls on the box in the center aisle, stood a very erect copper-colored bird. Though it was too early for the sun to invade the barn directly, the bird's feathers shimmered from copper to gold and back again as he probed the bowls for leftover treats with staccato movements of his head and neck.

The bird paused, stretched himself to his utmost, and, *"Eeeer-er-eerr-er-eerrrrrrrr!"*

The call fairly sparkled throughout the barn. A glorious sound! But then, the old rooster *knew* that.

Cat didn't know much about glorious sounds, but he did know bird meat when he saw it. And this one looked particularly tasty, dressed as it was in such feathered finery. The big cat did not feel compelled to make an attempt at stalking this bird, however, and that confused him. There was something within that made him hesitate. Many years had passed during which the creature had played a part in his life, though a minor one, to be sure. The rooster's announcements were part of Cat's memory, something familiar. Rooster's call lent a connecting thread from the marsh to the barn that permitted the cat a sense of security. He slowly lay down at the top of the stack of hay, to watch.

Lucky for Rooster.

His call and loud pecking noises upon the plastic bowl had aroused others as well as Cat. The sheep began moving in the pen beneath the hayloft, three horses clumped about restlessly in their stalls toward the front of the barn, and chickens clucked softly from their small house that hung on the barn's north wall. The little barn cat joined her large friend at his lookout, and lay down beside him to watch, and listen to the barn come to life.

Cat flinched noticeably when a small black cat jumped over a horse stall door and trotted across the floor. He strained forward, the better to see. Then another! Another cat, this one black with white paws, came from beneath them. From the sheep pen. It, too, trotted across the floor. And another, and another, till there were seven cats hanging about the barn floor in the vicinity of the wooden box that held their dishes.

The little gray barn cat got to her feet and began climbing down toward the loft floor. She stopped halfway, turned, and looked back at Cat. He did not move. His gaze remained fixed upon the main floor and its collection of other cats. She continued down, descended the stairs, and joined them. When she approached they greeted her with sniffs and body rubbing, obviously appreciating her appearance. After all, had she not been gone a day and a night? Certainly a first, for her.

The wild marsh cat watched quietly. He was not nervous. The sight of his little friend's acceptance and familiarity with these surroundings put him quite at ease. But he was very alert. Rarely during his life had he been

58

anything but alert. Where he came from, those who let their guard down do not survive.

The white-footed cat jumped upon the box, peeked into a bowl. Finding nothing, he returned to the floor. One cat, a particularly long-haired black one with but half a tail, walked over to the barn doors and poked his head outside. He watched for a moment, then quickly popped back inside, obviously excited.

He ran to the box and leaped upon it, then paced two or three times from one end to the other. The other cats became infected by his actions, and they, too, mounted the box. Then, the barn doors opened slightly!

Cat tensed, then his heart pounded. Through the narrow space between the doors walked a tall, two-legged thing! For an instant, Cat was paralyzed. He could not think. Could not move. The image of a bright flash coming from a tree, an exploding rock, and pain, all streaked through his brain at once.

The two-legged thing walked to the box, angrily shooed Rooster to the floor, and reached for a cat. Cat saw no more, for he disappeared from sight like a shadow in light. If he had stayed at his perch he would have seen another two-legs enter the barn.

"Daddy. Where's Thumbs?" she asked.

"I dunno, honey. He's prob'ly still sleepin' somewhere up there," said he, glancing at the beams overhead.

"Thumbs? Oh, Thumbs! Here, kitty, kitty, kitty."

"Tracy honey, I'll go get the water. Why don't you feed for me this morning? Hey! Wanna do that?"

"Oh, Daddy . . . Oh, okay, I guess so."

Cat lay within the hay cave listening to the voices with a pounding heart. If he had remained at his post he would have seen the man fondle several cats gently, and he would have seen a pretty, dark-haired girl pick up his gray friend and tuck her gently beneath her warm coat. She called her Puffer. Puffer looked forward to visits by Tracy, especially during colder days when she got to snuggle.

"Thumbs?"

"*Rrowwwwwwwr.*" An answer came from higher in the barn than where the wild cat lay.

"*Rrrowwwrrrr.*" A large yellow tiger cat walked slowly along a third-floor beam. Used to this precarious route, the old cat cut a corner, jumping from one beam to another. The only thing between him and the floor was thirty feet of open space. Thumbs's casual, friendly voice reached Cat's ears, and it eased his rapid heartbeat. He raised his head enough to see out across the upper barn, and caught glimpses of the big yellow cat as he jumped from beam to beam.

Cat crawled carefully to the edge of the hay, as carefully as he had ever crept through the marsh, and watched the cat Thumbs finally reach the floor and greet Tracy with rumbling purrs and surging side-rubs against her boots. Puffer's head poked from within the coat, and the little cat jumped to the floor, making quite a show of her affection for old Thumbs.

Tracy had a scoop of kibbles which she dumped into the orange bowls, and as soon as she did, her arm was buried in a sea of cats. Cat was hungry, but not hungry enough to—

She looked up! The girl looked up!

Again Cat vanished, like the shadow he was.

Tracy had seen something. A movement, maybe.

Cat lay within his hay bale lair, listening to the activities below. He heard the crunching of kibbles as the other cats wolfed down their breakfast. The horses made softer, more muffled sounds as they ate with their noses buried deep in large rubber buckets. The sheep made light brushing noises with their furry lips on the wooden trough as they stood side by side, each trying to be the one that trapped the last two grains of oat or corn.

The chickens? Well, they just pecked at dry meal. The only sound Cat heard from there was a casual scratching, as a hen turned over shavings on her floor, hoping to uncover some exotic treat. The chickens seemed always to carry on in a daze of eternal hope, when it came to food. "Tracy!" It was the two-legged Daddy thing's voice.

"Tracy . . . better hurry. Bus'll be here in a minute."

"Okay, Daddy." She always hated to leave the cats. School was certainly a poor substitute for a pile of friendly warm kitties.

Cat heard the barn doors close slowly. They were very heavy, and the wheels they hung from rumbled, vibrating the front wall of the barn.

After finishing their grain ration, the horses and sheep had been let out for the day, leaving the barn in comparative silence. Cat's settling nerves allowed him to doze off.

Puffer and the rest of the cats finished their morning meal, leaving quite a bit of food in the dishes. Tracy always gave them far more than they needed, and there was always plenty left for Rooster. Before the last cat had jumped from the box the gaudy bird was already pecking away, his disjointed plastic tattoo sounding quite like that of a drunken woodpecker.

Cat woke. Just as he did so, two furry faces peered over the top of the hay in front of him. One gray, one yellow.

At the sight of Thumbs's wide, scarred head, Cat's ears lay flat against his head, and muscles tensed. Neither cat moved. The old yellow cat was far larger than he had appeared at a distance, and he had *enormous* paws. Each had seven toes, with seven working claws. Thumbs had been the undisputed top of cat pecking order in this barn for many years. He didn't ever have to prove his physical superiority—the other cats *knew* they would lose in an argument with him!

Puffer stepped softly down, turned, and stood beside the tense Cat. The wild one was much larger than Thumbs, and certainly more adept at battle, but he was the outsider—always a mental disadvantage.

"*Rowrrrrrr.*" Thumbs uttered slowly. Puffer rubbed against Cat gently.

"*Rowrr.*" She began to purr loudly.

The black cat was disarmed by his confusion. He was ready to defend himself, attack, or flee, all at the same time. He was afraid of Thumbs, and he wasn't. Things in the marsh were more simple: eat and sleep. Here there were social complications he did not understand.

Gradually, Cat was put at ease by the constant attention of Puffer, and the fact that Thumbs was not at all aggressive. Puffer's obvious acceptance of the wild one had tempered Thumbs's natural tendency to defend his territory. His voice indicated he was simply interested in getting acquainted with this enormous creature. Thumbs had been around. It took a lot to unnerve him.

He stretched forward, gently nosing Cat's face: first from the tip of the nose to the eye, then down the jowl and forward again to the front of the mouth. The newcomer made no objection to any of the attentions, and by the time Thumbs had finished his investigation and settled back on his haunches Cat's nerves had reached a more normal state.

He became more and more at ease over the next several hours. The three cats lounged about high in the hay, cleaning, napping, rubbing, and generally indulging in feline vanities.

The barn was dimly lit from the opening between the doors, and from a small window high above them. The other cats had been long gone, pursuing their various daytime errands, most of which consisted of finding a nice place to spend a few hours sleeping.

Rooster had returned to the bowls several times to gulp down a few more kibbles. He liked warm weather better, for warm weather meant juicy morsels he would find in the yard: crickets, worms, and bugs of all kinds.

The barn had seemed very empty once the sheep and horses had left in the morning. Quiet, too. Now that the sun had risen, it sent the wind on little dances around the barn that made its bony frame move enough to creak. At first, Cat thought they were animal sounds, but accepted them as normal background when the other two cats failed to react.

The loft was becoming noticeably warmer now as the dark roof absorbed the rays of the sun. The roof was the first to melt bare after a snow. In the heat of summer the upper reaches of the barn were unbearably hot, to a point that no cat could stand to rest there. Even the bats retired to cooler haunts behind house shutters and deep within neatly stacked piles of stove wood.

Thumbs finally tired of just lying about. He was convinced this oversize visitor was not a threat to the stability of life in the barn. Convinced in his own way, that is. He simply was at ease with the fact that Cat was there.

He got up, climbed down to the main floor, and walked out the front door, just to see what the afternoon had to offer.

Puffer followed. Just before she went between the two doors she glanced back and up to the top of the hay. Cat was peeking over the edge intently, barely visible in the dimness of the loft. She twitched the tip of her tail, and delicately stepped out into the light.

Cat wanted to accompany them, for though he had lived a solitary life, being alone in this cavernous, unfamiliar place did make him uneasy. He returned to his bed and slept, slept and dreamed of fat, juicy grouse and coppery gold roosters.

Chapter Six

There was something afoot in the barn. Tracy knew that. Something different. Something new. Some *one* new.

She knew all the animals and had named most of them, even some of the sheep. The cats *all* had names.

Puffer was the oldest. She had given birth to so many kittens even Tracy could not remember how many there had been. The search and discovery of each new birthing nest was always a special time for her, and she missed it now. Daddy had gone and had Puffer fixed, finally. His excuse was that the old girl deserved a few years for herself. Tracy knew the *real* reason was that he got tired of spending so much time trying to find good homes for the kittens. She had managed to talk him into keeping a few of them over the years though.

He had gotten *all* the cats fixed! All at the same time. Figured he'd get a volume discount at the vet's. And he did.

Pieces was one of Puffer's kittens. He had lost half his tail and one ear in fights over the years, and in the spring, when he sheds his matted winter coat, he does look as though he is made of ragged pieces!

There is Oliver, the white-footed cat; Ives, who came from New Jersey; Crooky, a scaredy-cat with a tilted head; and Thumbs, of course. He arrived one day unannounced. Just walked up the lane from somewhere, and upon arriving at the barn, simply took over its management.

There were several cats labeled No-name. They were antisocial, too wild and skittery to allow human contact. They weren't even friends with the other cats.

Tracy knew exactly how much they ate. She knew how much Fred the rooster stole during the day. She also knew Fred did not eat at night.

Each morning before the school bus came she fed the cats. Now, ordinarily there was a good bit left over from the night before, because she always gave them too much—or at least, more than they needed.

But now there were *never* any leftovers.

During the next few weeks she became convinced the barn had a new resident. Not only was there never any leftover food, but if she entered the barn at an unexpected hour, any time other than feeding time, she would occasionally catch a fleeting glimpse of the shadow that was Cat, high in the loft, or farther up among the highest beams. Sometimes, after catching sight of him, she would sit on the stairs for a while, and wait. Cat slowly began to associate Tracy with the arrival of food. Though he certainly never joined the other cats when it was first delivered, he did sense their eagerness, and their confidence in the presence of the little girl. He would watch when they all crowded around her, and heard the gentleness in her voice as she spoke to each and every one in turn. He was *most* influenced by the affection shown her by Puffer and Thumbs.

Gradually he was slower to hide when she appeared through the doors. He could tell when Daddy was approaching the barn, for he clunked when he walked. If the snow was particularly soft he could *still* tell the difference between the two: Daddy opened the doors much faster. Daddy *never* caught sight of Cat!

In the beginning.

Late one night in early January, after he had finished off the last of the kibbles, Cat sat on the main floor facing the front of the barn, cleaning himself. Tracy had forgotten to close the doors, and moonlight reflected off the snow into the barn. Puffer was crouched in front of the feed room door listening intently to the mice that crept through a crack in the floor every night and stuffed themselves with corn and oats. They knew she was behind the door. They didn't care.

Suddenly, Daddy appeared! Cat hadn't heard him come. No crunching snow. No rumbling doors. His heart froze.

For an instant.

Then adrenaline flooded.

Without a step or a scramble, the cat sprang to the loft floor and vanished!

The man was stunned. He thought he saw what he saw but he couldn't have! There weren't any cats that big! Tracy had told him about seeing a huge cat, but he'd chalked it up to a little girl's imagination. It couldn't be, but it *was*.

He went over to the wall and raised his hand up to the level of the loft floor. That cat had jumped seven and a half feet, without touching the wall!

He knew there was no chance of spotting the creature again, so with more than just a little sense of wonder he shut the doors and returned to the house.

Some cat!

Tracy was some old pleased. He told her of the event the next morning, and that day in school she could think of nothing else but Cat. She knew by then he had been around for over a month, so he would probably stay in the barn for the rest of the winter. The snow was deep now. He certainly wouldn't leave the comfort of the barn and regular meals at this time of year.

When she got home that afternoon, Tracy changed into her barn clothes and tackled her main chore: loading the wood boxes in the house. The four trips to the woodpile seemed to take forever! Finally finished, she took a banana from the fruit basket and hurried to the barn. The temperature was falling rapidly now that the sun was going down, and she found it hard to take deep breaths. Within an hour or two it would be twenty below—no time to be gulping air.

She opened the doors as quietly as possible, slid through, and closed them.

She then lay down on her back in the middle of the central aisle and peeled the banana. Tracy had done this same thing many times out in the woods with her father.

He had shown her that animals usually don't recognize humans when they are lying down. Some are very curious, and if the wind is right and they can't identify the person by smell, then often the animal will come quite close, if you don't move.

Cat was lying at his customary lookout high in the loft when Tracy entered the barn, and he pulled back out of sight when she first came in. The customary noises of feeding did not commence, nor did she talk to the other cats, as was her habit when she came to the barn.

He listened, trying to figure out what was happening down below, and after a few moments of silence crept back to the edge of the hay. He saw a bundled-up form lying on the floor. A form quite different from most two-legged things. It lay there quiet and still, and he felt in no way threatened, even when it moved now and then to take a bite of banana.

Tracy's head was turned slightly toward the right, but her eyes strained up and to the left as she watched Cat, watching her.

It was the first time she had actually had a clear view of him, and even though the only thing she could see was his head, her heart raced. The muscles behind her eyes ached with the effort. It was a relief when Puffer climbed upon her stomach and lay down, grateful to spend some time on a warm, person-mattress. Tracy moved her banana hand slowly up over the little cat, stroked her gently, and Puffer responded with a purr. Cat heard the sound clearly, and edged farther forward.

He watched as Puffer took full, delicious advantage of her position, flattening herself upon Tracy's down parka, soaking up every bit of heat that escaped through the fabric.

Thumbs wandered over, and upon investigating the possibilities, climbed up on Tracy's legs and curled himself there. Tracy lay very still now, enjoying the company of the two cats, but still straining to see the big black cat high in the loft who was watching her.

Cat was again calmed somewhat by the familiarity with which his two friends regarded the girl. Every visit she paid to the barn was an opportunity for them to get

rubbed or fed, or both. They looked forward to her appearances, that was obvious, and Cat sensed it. He crept a bit farther out along the bale and lay down, stretched full-length along its very edge, the better to watch.

When she saw the size of the complete cat Tracy could only wonder, thinking that this must be the biggest cat in the whole world! The bales were about three feet long, and that cat was almost as long, without its tail! They watched each other. Tracy hoped Cat would move and give her an even better view. He didn't.

He just watched.

The other cats began to assemble slowly. They came from under the barn where they had spent the day investigating mousy places. They were not terribly adventurous cats. Maybe they would have been if food didn't automatically appear twice a day. But it did, so frigid winter hunts did not enter their minds. Thumbs, in particular, might have been very happy to have a winter home in Florida! He was usually the first to take advantage of whatever comforts presented themselves.

"*Rowrrrr.*" He complained, as Tracy shifted her weight slightly. *She* was getting chilled now, in spite of her heavy clothing. The temperature was reaching a more cruel level outside and began seeping through the floorboards beneath her. She shivered. She hated to move. The big cat had shifted himself several times during her vigil, and she had really gotten a thorough look at him. Now she wanted desperately to spend more time in the barn to see if she could get closer.

Maybe even touch him.

Cat shrank back over the horizon of hay as soon as Tracy moved Puffer onto the floor, and as she raised up on her elbow to give Thumbs a pat, Cat vanished back into the maze of bales, this time at a more leisurely pace than ever before.

Feed time. Feed time. Homework time, too. She grained the horses and sheep, filled the sheep's hay crib to the limit, and ladled an extra large amount of kibbles into the two cat dishes. After getting a good look at the new cat Tracy *knew* the food would all be gone in the morning. She knew, and it was.

January. The cold month. The creatures held in the ancient hand-hewn embrace of the winter barn drew small breaths as they waited for warmer days. The snow piled deep, until only a long-legged creature like Horse could move about at will.

The cats sunned themselves on the hard-packed snow outside the big barn doors for a few brief hours before the sun set behind the trees, and the sheep huddled together in a compact mass, providing each other with heat. They heated others, too.

Rooster spent the nights perched on top of his own woolly furnace, and Oliver did it, too. Once the sheep had settled for the night he would sneak through the slats of the hay crib and carefully climb on top of a ewe, find the most level spot, and curl up till Rooster awakened them all.

January was bitter cold. Cat became gradually more bold, more confident of the workings and schedule of barn life, and during the day, when Tracy was at school and the Daddy was absent, he would feel free to explore.

He knew the loft well. He knew every alley and hidden nook between the bales. There was a shop full of lumber on the opposite side of the loft where mice tried to travel undetected beneath boards and stacked boxes of nails, paint, and stuff. Stuff. Just stuff left over from projects over the years.

On the first floor by the front of the barn was the feed room. Cat could hear mice and an occasional rat romping in there during the night, safe from cats. Safe behind a latched door.

In the back of the barn, alongside the sheep pen, there were two tractors, a big wooden horse cart, some piles of chains on the floor, and assorted small machinery. Cat didn't know what they were, he just knew there wasn't any comfortable place to bed down back there. Cold, hard stuff. None of the cats liked cold, hard stuff.

Toward the end of the month the ewes began to get restless. Thumbs had been sleeping on one or another of them during quite a number of the colder nights. Cat was curious about that, and finally followed him to see what the attraction was. Thumbs climbed between the two bottom boards, but Cat simply stuck his head through and watched. The sheep were all lying down chewing their cuds, eyes half-closed. Thumbs proceeded to the nearest one, and without hesitation, climbed carefully to its back. There was no reaction from the ewe other than a contented *"Mu-u-uh."*

Cat watched for a moment, then slipped through the space in the boards. These were larger animals than he had ever been in close contact with, and upon entering the pen he sat next to the fence. And watched. The sheep seemed like docile creatures, but they did smell pretty bad. In spite of that, Cat crept close to a particularly sleepy one. She took no notice of him, as she was used to all manner of cats taking advantage of her warmth over the years. The fact that this one was three or four times their size didn't register as any kind of a threat, and she allowed him to approach. He sniffed at her, over her, around her, and, satisfied she was as docile as she appeared, he put his two front paws high on her distended side and looked over the top of her.

He didn't like the spongy feel of the thick, greasy fleece, but was *very* attracted to the warmth he felt flowing from it. Carefully he lay down beside her. Cat didn't care for the smell of the sheep, nor did he like the smell of the compacted straw on the floor, but this was the warmest January night he had ever spent.

During the next few days the Daddy came to the barn more often, checking the sheep pen and looking at the woolly animals very carefully. Cat omitted his daytime prowling of the barn now, for he never knew when that two-legged one would appear through the door. Though he had become somewhat more at ease with the little girl, the sight of the taller Daddy chilled him to the core. Except for Thumbs and Puffer, the other cats were even skittery when he came around.

One night the ewe Thumbs had been using for a mattress became somewhat ill at ease. Her nervousness woke him, and when she began grunting he took his leave, joining Cat alongside his ewe. They both watched intently as the restless one got up, walked about, and lay down.

She did this a number of times before she lay down for the last time and began to breath in labored grunts. The grunts did it! Both Thumbs and Cat lit out for the hayloft. The yellow cat pursued his regular rounds the next day, but Cat stayed aloft. The Daddy was in and out of the barn several times in quick succession the next morning, making any forays onto the main floor impossible for Cat.

Tracy came twice before the school bus arrived in the morning, and the cat sensed her excitement when she blurted out, "Daddy! Daddy! Two lambs! Oh, Daddy, do I *have* to go to school today?"

Cat watched from high above them as the Daddy put his arm around Tracy and said something in a very soft, low voice.

"Oh, Daddy . . . Oh, oka-a-ay."

She took a moment to watch the sheep pen, then slowly walked out of the barn.

Thumbs had gone downstairs before Tracy left. So had Puffer. Cat saw them sitting by the fence, intent upon the activity within the pen. He was curious, but no way was he going to show himself while the two-legged thing was around. His recollection of the exploding rock was dim in his memory now, but distrust for two-leggeds lingered, keeping his survival senses well honed.

During that day the wind gathered strength, and as it gradually changed course from the south and began boring in from the northwest it brought first a hint of snow, then the concentration of flakes increased until there seemed to be no spaces between them. The air outside the barn became a swirling cloud of white, and visibility was reduced to a few feet. Little piles of snow began building up wherever the wind found a chink in the barn's wooden armor, and in the front of the barn it blew unencumbered through the space between the doors, forming a great drift down the center aisle. The cats were uneasy. They had never seen snow blowing this hard into the barn before.

The Daddy came to the barn any number of times that day. He shoveled snow from the floor twice during the storm and went into the sheep pen several times to make sure the newborn lambs were feeding properly. He set up two heat lamps in the corner to help keep them warm, and checked the other ewes to see if they were close to their birthing time. Cat kept track of all this from Thumbs's favorite third-floor beam.

The big cat's fears were gradually overpowered this day by his interest in the new activity taking place below. He knew the Daddy had seen him once, when he glanced up and held Cat's gaze in his own for the span of a breath. The cat did not feel threatened.

After Tracy returned from school she appeared, bundled as before, and spent the rest of the afternoon in the sheep pen with the lambs.

Once she had entered the pen Cat couldn't see her from the loft, so he climbed down and joined Puffer on the landing at the top of the stairs. From there they both could see Tracy sitting on the floor next to the two newborns. The lambs were curled up, lying back to back beneath the suspended heat lamps. They were snug and warm, despite the cold that hovered beyond the lamp's warm glow. Every so often their mother approached and nuzzled the babies from stem to stern. She nuzzled Tracy, too, for the odor of lambs was on her hands and lingered about her clothes. She held very still when the ewe came near.

Thumbs sidled from beneath one of the tractors, climbed through the fence, and joined the little group beneath the lamps. Tracy thought he was coming to socialize. Really what he wanted was a little of that lovely lamp heat for himself!

Cat heard scraping noises beyond the barn doors. He knew that meant the Daddy was making a new path between the house and barn, and would soon appear, so the cat retired to the loft.

Tracy heard, too, and got up reluctantly. It was past time to feed.

Before she left the barn, the girl noticed that two more ewes had started pacing—and she knew what *that* meant!

By the time Tracy and her father had left the barn the assorted cats had polished off at least half of the kibbles. Rooster was up on the box as well, poking first at a grain of food, then at a cat, trying to bully them from what he thought was his own private food supply. His comb jiggled in indignation when they refused to react, and he poked again and again till the various little cats jumped to the floor. Plenty left for Rooster.

"Errr-er-er-er-eerrrrrr!"

Then Cat returned to the main floor and jumped to the box for his share. Rooster stood straight for a moment, regarding Cat with baleful eye as the newcomer crunched great mouthfuls of the hard, dry bits. His comb began to jiggle.

The cat finished what was in the left-hand bowl, and began eating from the other. Rooster looked into the empty bowl and delivered a quick peck to retrieve the solitary crumb remaining. He then looked at Cat scarfing up the other food, and with a sudden flutter of wings lifted himself from the box and with his feet discharged half a dozen sharp blows to the shoulder of Cat!

The big cat flinched in surprise, and crouched instinctively, facing the rooster. The feisty bird lowered his head, hackle feathers spread to their fullest, and with comb a-jiggle he launched at Cat again.

Big mistake.

When the bird flashed into range, Cat flicked out a paw, hooked a wing, and with both front feet pinned the hapless rooster to the boards.

Many grouse had met their end in this position! The cat's first instinct was to eat the bird. But he was already full of food, and besides, Rooster did not smell at all appetizing. In fact, he was a pretty stinky bird. Pretty, but stinky!

Cat opened his mouth wide, exposing a frightful array of teeth, and at the same time let out a half growl-half hiss that shocked the other cats to attention. Then, with a powerful sweep of his paw, he hurled Rooster from the box, sending him tumbling to the opposite side of the center aisle. The bird hit the wall with a dull thud and fell to the floor. Rooster righted himself, ruffled his feathers noisily into place, and stalked off with a high-stepping lurch and a slight limp, to regain his dignity in a more private place.

Cat cleaned up the remaining cat food, probably as a matter of principle.

Later that evening Tracy returned to the barn. She had convinced her parents to let her wait up for a few hours, on the chance a lamb would be born. She had never seen it happen. In her argument she stressed the educational aspect of such an experience. They just smiled and said, "Fine."

It was *very* cold by that time, and she bundled up as never before: two pair of wool socks beneath felt-lined boots, long underwear, a pair of sweatpants under heavy wool pants, a sweatshirt over a wool shirt, and a down parka over that. On her hands was a pair of deerskin mittens with wool liners, and on her head was a thick watch cap made from their own sheep's wool. She snuck a banana in her pocket and headed out.

The cats were still hanging about when she entered the barn. Puffer and Thumbs were in with the lambs, the others lounged at the top of the stairs. It was their habit to socialize before retiring for the night. Cat was still on the box when Tracy came through the door.

His back was to her. When he heard the first footstep upon the wooden floor he leaped to the stairs and jumped to the landing. He crouched behind the assembled cats and watched, as the girl stared at the group.

Her best view yet! Even though he was hunkered down as far as he could go there still was a lot of Cat to see.

She watched for a moment, then, not wanting to intimidate him, she moved slowly along the opposite wall toward the sheep pen. The cats followed her with their eyes till she was out of sight. Cat made no attempt to flee for cover.

Tracy climbed into the hay crib to wait for The Great Event, and lay full-length upon it. The sound of the sheep was comforting, the heat from the nearby lamps took the edge off the frigid air, and before she realized she was drowsy, Tracy was sound asleep.

Cat waited for over an hour before he descended the stairs to join Thumbs and Puffer in the sheep pen. The other cats were long in their beds, and he was feeling the chill. He climbed through the fence and joined the heat lamp group, unaware of the sleeping girl overhead, scant feet away.

Now and then one of the lambs would utter a faint *"M-a-a,"* but Cat was getting used to that now. He was *not* used to having a ewe approach him closely. When one came over in response to her baby's call, and the little lamb staggered to his feet, Cat hustled under the hay crib and watched from there as the lamb tottered along the ewe's side searching for his meal. When he reached her udder he responded with much head thrusting, punching and butting to make the milk flow freely.

Two other ewes were on the floor panting and grunting, preparatory to giving birth, and Tracy slept through it all.

Two sets of twins were born during the next two hours. All were licked clean by their mothers, but the second to be born from each set did not arrive as lively as its twin. The two firstborns were on their feet in less than an hour, searching for milk. The other two lay far from the lamp, close together, but shivering from the cold. Cat watched.

In the crib over Cat's head the sleeping girl altered her position slightly, and he cringed in alarm, ready to flee. Her mittened hand slid between the slats overhead. He hesitated, raised himself slightly, and sniffed the tip of the mitten: It smelled like lambs. No threat there. He was reassured by her steady breathing, and settled himself back on the straw beneath her, to watch.

"Tracy honey . . . Tracy. Wake up, honey."

Cat froze.

The Daddy was here!

When he entered the pen all Cat could see through the screen of hay hanging in front of the crib was the bottom half of two long legs! Two legs. Daddy legs! Cat's heart raced.

"Damn!" The man exclaimed when he saw the two abandoned lambs. "Damned old ewes."

He picked up the two shivering forms and placed them gently beside the other two under the lamps. "Shoo, cats!" At that, Thumbs and Puffer left the pen, quickly.

"Wake up, Trace." He repeated softly.

The big cat remained rigid, unseen beneath the crib, as her father picked the little girl up in his arms.

"Oh, Daddy, more lambs." Then she was asleep again, and footsteps told Cat the barn was his.

He crept toward the two abandoned lambs, carefully, lest a ewe might think him a threat to her own. He smelled them carefully from head to toe, and for no reason known to him, lay down across one and began licking the face of the other. He started over the top of its eye, and when he had worked his way down the face to just under the chin the delicate little animal uttered a faint *"Maaa . . ."*

During the next three days, Tracy and her father returned to the barn every four hours to bottle-feed the abandoned lambs, and each time, or rather, each time they managed to sneak into the barn quietly, they discovered the huge, black cat lying with the lambs. When they appeared the first time he leaped frantically from the pen and hid far back in the center aisle under the machinery. They did not seek him out. On each successive visit the cat seemed to exit with slightly less haste, but exit he surely did! They made a point of not pressing him once he was out of the pen, though Tracy wanted desperately to get as close as she could to him. Her father cautioned that it could only make Cat withdraw more.

The lambs were finally coaxed to feed from a bucket with several nipples attached, and that ended the constant invasions into Cat's nervous system.

He had grown fond of the lambs, fond of the warmth beneath the lamps, and especially fond of the formula mix in the nippled bucket! It was attached firmly to a large post, and was just the right height for Cat. If he stood on his hind legs and held the rim with his forepaws, he could reach his head almost halfway down inside. It was warm and rich. A welcome addition to the dried stuff in the cat bowls.

The only cats who ventured with him into the sheep pen were Puffer and Thumbs, and they were not big enough to reach into the bucket. So when Cat finished he lay down with them under the light and they each licked the drop or two he might have spilled on his glossy, black coat. Sometimes he was neat, and the disappointment showed in their eyes.

A week passed, and Cat became used to the comings and goings of Tracy. Never her father. She could come to the pen and stand by the fence quietly, and he would not move from under the lamp. Thumbs would always greet her with a *"Rowrrr."* If Puffer was there she would rub the girl's legs and purr a request for a warm, soft lap.

By the time a dozen more lambs had been born the pen became not quite so peaceful a place. Very noisy. *Very* noisy, and smellier, too. Cat became used to the jostling and sounds of the little voices as they called for a meal or complained of the cold. At a month of age the lambs seemed to develop coil springs in their legs. That's what they did—without any notice at all they could spring! Spring! Spring!... All four legs in the air at

82

once! Cat found himself ducking from time to time when courses went awry.

Cat and Thumbs slept with the lambs, for the heat lamps were a constant lure. Sometimes on top, sometimes buried beneath a pile of kinky bodies, the two cats slept warm and sound.

One night quite late—it must have been a weekend night—Tracy came to the pen and no one awoke. Oh, there was a sleepy sound from a lamb or two, or a quiet complaint from an old ewe, but those were natural sounds. She saw Cat, half-buried beneath some lambs, just his head and a shoulder showed . . . and part of a hind leg.

She held her breath and reached out slowly through the fence, then withdrew her hand quickly when Cat flicked an ear! She tried again. This time she laid her fingers gently upon his shoulder. He flicked a whisker, perhaps dreaming of Squirrel, or even Frog, then Owl. He opened an eye slowly. He felt the pressure of lambs all around, and the pulse of a half-dozen tiny hearts, then he saw the face Thumbs and Puffer loved so well, framed in a sheep's wool hat. His heart remained steady. Cat was warm, and his eye slowly closed again.

Tracy visited the barn whenever she could during the next few weeks, to play with lambs and to look at Cat. He was usually in the pen, and, if Thumbs or Puffer were with him, he never appeared to be afraid when she approached. She often reached through to pet the two tame cats, and would carefully move her hand softly over the big one when he became distracted by a lamb or ewe. It happened often. She never pressed him if she thought his mood was anything other than receptive, and his nerves responded: He no longer felt threatened. At least by the little girl. The Daddy was quite a different matter.

One night, during the January thaw, a night of unaccustomed warmth, the population of cats was lounging about the landing at the top of the stairs when Tracy came to feed. Cat was there, too. She fed the horses and sheep, filled the cat bowls, then walked slowly up the stairs, talking all the while to Puffer and Thumbs. The big cat shrank back a bit as her head rose above the level of the landing. He backed slowly, without taking his eyes off her, until his rear pressed against the storeroom wall. The unexpected pressure sent his heart rate to pounding, but he did not try to flee.

Tracy did not look at him, rather, she turned around slowly, and very carefully sat down on the landing. Immediately Puffer and Thumbs demanded attention, purring and rubbing, making quite a display.

The other cats wanted to *eat*! One by one they squeezed by, and walked down the stairs.

Cat raised up from his crouch and sat watching the three carrying on in front of him. Tracy leaned back, propping herself on her elbows, and the two cats promptly climbed on top of her and arranged themselves comfortably.

The gentleness he had witnessed up to this point conditioned Cat to forget about threats, and he became finally convinced that no dangers lurked within this little girl.

Cat got to his feet, and walked carefully toward her. He made no sound.

When he was close enough he stretched, and balancing almost all his weight on his forelegs, and sniffed the back of her arm. Thumbs craned his neck and watched, as Cat explored the back of the girl tentatively with nose and whisker.

She smelled like sheep, she smelled like food, and she smelled like cats. Lots of cats. Sprinkled among those familiar smells was a little trace of Girl, as well.

She knew he was there, and she did not move.

The big cat rose to his normal height, assembled his various feline dignities, and, picking his way delicately past the three companions, descended the stairs.

Tracy's heart jumped to her throat as she became aware the cat was walking by! Afraid to move her head, lest she frighten him, she strained her eyes to the side. Cat walked by close enough to rub against her arm, then her side. Thumbs slid his cheek along a great, black shoulder as it passed, and just as Cat placed his foot down on the first step Tracy moved her hand. With the back of it she felt the glossy, black fur gliding by.

Cat was aware of the hand, and as it slid over his tail he turned his head, looking the girl full in the eye.

He was not afraid.

Chapter Seven

The warmer weather of the past few days had made Cat restless. The boring kibbles that appeared each day made him restless, too. A top had been put on the orphan lamb's bucket. The Daddy said too much was being sampled by Cat, and too much *was*. He had developed a layer of fat beneath his skin, a malady more common in his domestic kin.

One morning, after Rooster had made his pronouncements for the day, Cat heard Crow chuckling off in the distance, off toward the marsh. As much as he liked the comfort of the barn, the friendship of Thumbs and Puffer and Tracy's touch, he missed the solitude of his former life. He missed the clean smell of fir trees in the rain, and he missed sweet water that bubbled from the ground.

Crow spoke again, reminding Cat of the freedoms they shared beyond these walls: to prowl, to hunt, to watch a working party of beavers toil. He had been content with kibbles and milk, but now he thought of meals of fat, juicy grouse.

That night, after the barn was asleep and nothing

stirred, Cat walked out through the great front doors. He headed directly along the wall that had led him here, the night he and Puffer arrived. He saw the glow in the window at the back of the house, but it didn't bother him now. The snow had melted during the long days of thaw. Only patches remained: tokens of the harsher days of cutting winds and short, quick breaths. Cat walked with an easy stride across dampened leaves, pine needles, and lichened rocks.

Quietly.

He leaped over the wall that led to the birches, and headed directly into deep pine woods. He had gone but a few feet when he heard a sound, and stopped. He listened. Just the squeak of a limb rubbing on another that belonged to a sister tree. Hare and Grouse beckoned beyond the pines, back in the dark spruce woods, and Cat continued on at a somewhat domestic, clumsy trot. He was not afraid.

Deeper snow now, but soft, sometimes a bit too moist to suit the cat. He was in the spruce, where Hare foraged wide and sometimes a grouse was foolish enough to roost too low. Kibbles seemed a distant meal as Cat crept from beneath a low spruce bough, and stopped.

Before him, in a six-foot clearing between three trees, an object hung from a string overhead. He had never seen such a thing before. It looked like a stick, or perhaps a bone, and hung suspended four feet high above the snow.

This was a puzzle. It did not fit into the scheme of natural things. It was an intrusion: almost an exclamation mark in the surrounding softness of dimly lit, furry trees. Cat regarded the object at the end of the string with a curious eye.

He approached the string, circling slowly, so as to better examine all sides of the object it held. A log lay a few inches beneath the snow, creating a low ridge that ran directly across the center of the clearing. Cat climbed upon it and approached the stick. Upon closer scrutiny it was not a stick at all, but rather, a dried bone. There were brittle splinters of dried meat attached firmly to the lower end, and they had little odor. Just enough to spark Cat's interest.

He stepped closer, and stood erect on his hind legs to measure the distance. The bone hung low enough for him to reach with forelegs outstretched. The cat raised himself again. This time he grasped the bone and tried to pull it down, but the branch it was tied to was too springy, and the string wouldn't break. He let it go, and the bone whipped into the air as if from a slingshot, then returned to its original position above the log, gently bobbing . . . beckoning.

Cat had slipped from the log when he released the bone, and he now stood on the ground, frustrated. But briefly.

Determined to have that bone, the cat remounted the log and approached again. He stood up, grasped the bone with his paws, pulled it toward him, and this time he took a firm hold with his teeth as well. Thus solidly attached, he threw his whole weight into the effort.

The branch bent to its limit, stiffened, and gave cat the resistance he needed. He tugged hard, his neck and back muscles straining to break the string as he fought to stay balanced on the log. Suddenly he heard a muffled *click*. Something shocked Cat hard on his right hind leg, but for a second or two he was so intent on recovering the bone that the blow didn't register. Then he felt a resistance there. He was caught in something. He had been stuck or caught in and under things a few times in his life, so this prompted no particular reaction other than annoyance.

Still firmly grasping the bone, Cat shook his leg hard, to free it from its burden. Then a slash of pain shot up his leg! A pain like no other he had ever experienced—more than exploding rocks or talons of Owl. He tumbled from the log with explosive snarls, convulsively shaking his captive leg. Snow, bark, and spruce needles flew, as the panicked cat struggled to escape.

A small steel trap held him fast. A trap that was meant for Fisher. Fisher: the next to largest member of the weasel family at fifteen pounds and more, whose luxurious black coat makes him a prime target in the trapping trade. The others had been taken up by the trapper at the end of the season, but this one lay forgotten, improperly charted and left behind. The bone on the string had been his bait, but the only thing it nourished had been woodpeckers and cold winter air. Now the bone hung high over the wounded cat, taunting . . .

In absolute panic, Cat twisted his body like an eel on a line, twisting the chain that held him fast. The links kinked, drawing him closer to the anchoring log till the trap was hard against solid wood. With great effort he pushed against the log with his free left leg. The jaws of the rusty trap ripped down his right, scraping hair and skin from the fragile bone.

Still held fast, the wounded cat lay on his side panting, uncomprehending.

The trap had pulled down to the top of his foot, and the jaws closed tighter as they came in contact with the smaller bones. His leg burned where the skin had ripped, but there was little loss of blood. The pain was minor now, compared to the terror of being trapped, the terror of the unknown.

Cat tried to move his leg again, and upon feeling the resistance of the trap on his foot he flew into a rage, biting and scraping at the offending piece of metal. One of his teeth broke in half, exposing the nerve, and the pain from it seared his brain. He fell back again, exhausted.

Cat lay there for over an hour. The melting snow beneath him soaked slowly into his fur, chilling him thoroughly. He found that so long as he didn't move his leg, the pain in his foot was bearable. The circulation to his toes had been cut off by the trap. The nerves were torn and deadened. The nerve in his tooth was not!

Fisher had been prowling about before Cat blundered into the trap that had been meant for *him*. He was lurching through the snow intent on a dinner of porcupine, his favorite food, when he heard the snarls of the trapped cat. The voice was familiar, and well it might have been. For when Porcupine had been scarce, Fisher dined many times on house cats who strayed too often into the deep woods at night. Their snarls were similar to the ones he just heard, perhaps a bit higher in tone.

He struck off boldly toward the sounds he had heard. Caution was not a part of Fisher's hunt. He was relentless and bold in the pursuit of prey, chasing them down on the ground or in trees, unafraid, for there was nothing in these woods that could challenge his murderous nature.

As he neared the clearing, Fisher took to the trees, jumping from one to another on an overlapping branch. Clumps of snow fell to the ground along the way, making whispery sounds as they broke up on boughs below.

Cat heard. Through the haze of confusion and pain that beset him, he heard.

His senses peaked. He turned on his side to face the sound, and the movement made his trapped foot ache sharply. He could not stand. The tightly twisted links had effectively bound the trap securely against the log.

Fisher was close now. He heard the clink of chain as Cat moved, trying to focus through pained, golden eyes. He jumped from the branch to the end of the log where it disappeared beneath the tree, and stopped. From where he stood he could see the trapped cat clearly.

Cat! To fisher, no more than an easy meal. But, like Owl, he failed in his judgement of relative size, and launched himself boldly to the attack.

Cat had seen the sleek animal drop to the log. He knew he was in danger and tried to bring his body around to face the threat. Just as he was raising up on his good front legs, the fisher struck, knocking the big cat sideways to the snow. He sank his teeth into Cat's neck and they rolled twice over in a flurry of teeth and claws.

With his right foreclaws Cat ripped four deep furrows in his foe's left side, and the surprise of it made Fisher loose his grip. His fury didn't allow him to feel the pain, but all four wounds dripped steadily, reddening the snow.

When they rolled on the ground some links unwound, and Cat found himself able to stand. The intruder hesitated at the unexpected size of the beast before him, but true to his kind, he attacked again with no less of an effort than before.

This time the exhausted cat was ready. The fisher attacked, and Cat sank eight foreclaws deep, pulling the screaming animal close. He sank his teeth beneath the jowl, effectively closing off Fisher's air, and with convulsive movements of his powerful hind legs raked Fisher in the lower regions till he resembled nothing more than ribbons of red.

Cat lay still for some moments on the blood-soaked ground, the dead animal clutched tightly in his grip. Gradually his heart slowed, and pain replaced fury as he became more aware of his broken tooth and mangled foot.

The foot! He was free.

When Cat's hind legs were brought to bear he had jerked with such force that his toes tore free. He disentangled himself from the body of Fisher and tried to sit up. As he did so, a wave of dizziness forced him back to the ground, and warm nausea flooded his throat. He shifted his body, and looked at the foot. Or at the toe that was left. Three had remained in the jaws of the trap.

Cat couldn't reach the punctures in his neck, but he could curl himself enough to reach the foot, which he did, licking clean all traces of dirt, and Fisher.

Hunger was far from his mind just now. Shelter. Shelter was what he needed most.

Cat struggled slowly to his three good legs, and shuffled wearily along the length of the log. At the opposite end from where Fisher had come it continued on, under a spruce tree and out the other side. The tree was a blowdown, and at its far end an uprooted stump reached roots to the sky. There Cat found crude shelter, absent of snow, between three small boulders that had failed to hold roots during a storm.

He crawled stiffly in, did his best to curl in a comfortable way, and slept.

Chapter Eight

"Errr-er-er-er-errrrrrrrrrr."

Cat stirred at the sound of the familiar call.

He had not slept well at all. His tooth ached sharply still, and the mangled foot just plain hurt. It had stopped leaking blood, but each time he altered his position slightly, the pain of it made him wince.

During the battle his fur had collected bits of snow which melted during the night, soaking him to the skin, and though it was not terribly cold, spasms of shivering overtook him from time to time.

Cat raised his head slowly. The punctures in his neck were not painful, but his muscles were stiff and sore, making that simple movement an effort he did not want to repeat.

He passed the day drifting in and out of sleep, trying not to move. Now and again a nagging pebble or root beneath him would force a shift of position, reawakening each ache and pain.

By evening Cat was overtaken by alternating waves of heat and cold. His fur had dried, but the chills that gripped him could not be held at bay by a mere coat of fur. Utter exhaustion had lowered his resistance, and his system was all but defenseless against infection from his wounds. The torn foot was not the cause. Fisher's claws and teeth were as septic as anything in the woods, and the bacteria that clung to them invaded Cat's body unopposed.

He lay between the rocks, drifting in and out of consciousness, with images of lambs, fishers, gentle cats, and little girls swirling about his clouded mind. He struggled through the night, and the following day as well.

Cat had never been ill, nor had he ever been anything but clear and alert. Now, disabled by wounds and infection, his mind clouded with fever, the big cat was confused. During lucid moments that touched him briefly he felt hunger and loneliness.

And fear.

Deep within him the instinct for survival smoldered still, making him feel vulnerable where he lay. It made him acknowledge insecurity and fear, and it forced images of warm cats, soft words, and caves in the hay upon him.

It was dark again when that instinct took over his body and made him rise, and he emerged from under the stump in a daze, his weakened body crying out from every muscle and joint to be left behind. Left alone. Left alone . . . to die.

Cat walked slowly, hampered by the pain in his crippled hind foot, barely aware that in bits and pieces the ground was slowly moving beneath him. The log led him past the crumpled body of Fisher, but Cat did not notice.

He retraced his route of two nights before quite by

coincidence, following the natural flow of the terrain that created the easiest path through the spruce woods. When he came to the pine though, a familiar series of sounds reached through to him.

Drumming. Clumping. The sounds of horse's feet on the wooden barn floor as they impatiently awaited the arrival of evening grain.

Cat faced the sounds. He forced his two front feet to move, supported his weight over them, then hopped his left rear foot forward. Right front, left front, and hop. Right, left, and hop. With the completion of each labored series Cat moved eight inches closer to safety. Unlike within the dense thickets of spruce, the snow cover in the pines was all but gone now and each carefully placed step met with solid ground, giving Cat a definite measure of progress, and contact with the world outside his muddled brain. Then, a muffled rumble: The barn doors had been closed for the night. He was still headed in the right direction.

The cat struggled on, inch by inch. At times he stumbled and almost fell, and had he done so, most probably he would have eventually died on that spot. Keep moving. Survive. These were not things he could consciously do. They were instinctive: compulsions dictated by a courageous heart.

Cat dragged himself through a gap in the wall that ran along the back of the house, and once through he was encouraged onward by the warm flood of light from the kitchen window.

The journey from there to the barn that had taken only minutes the first time Puffer led him there, now took over an hour. Cat finally reached the opening in the barn

foundation, and with his forelegs dragged the upper half of his body through the hole. For a moment he lay there, exhausted.

Little made any sense to Cat at this point. He had no rational thought, just a strong urge to be safe. He struggled on, dragging his lower half clear of the ancient stones. Raising himself on his front legs, he then tried to collect his good hind leg beneath him, but it would not obey. He fell sideways against a roll of rusty chicken wire, and fell to the ground.

After a moment's rest the cat again raised himself in the front. Barely conscious, he followed the pattern of his first entry into the barn, struggling up the grade toward the front, drawn to the sounds of hooves on wood. He bumped his head hard on an oaken beam, but barely noticed. His subconscious did. It forced him to the right, leading him, goading him to crawl between two beams that led to the foundation wall. By now Cat was not aware enough to see, but the texture of hay against his chest told him he was safe.

Chapter Nine

Tracy was disappointed not to see Cat when she came to feed that first morning after he had left the barn. She had really been counting on touching him again. When she went to bed the night before she thought about him a lot. She wondered how long it would be before she could actually hold him in her lap. She tried to imagine how it would feel to have a cat that *big* in her lap! Or under her jacket, or . . . maybe even curled up on her bed, or . . . the *or*'s went on and on, till she finally fell asleep.

First she looked in the sheep pen, then went up to the loft and searched in every nook and cranny. She knew them all well. No mother cat had ever successfully hidden a litter of kittens from Tracy. Thumbs and Puffer were there, as always, and the other cats were just hanging around. But nowhere could she find a trace of the big black cat.

The school bus came.

That night she searched again. No Cat. The next day was Saturday. She looked in every spot she had covered during her previous efforts, and even struggled a ladder to the woodshop floor and climbed overhead to the third floor level where Thumbs used to sleep. Nothing up there but a stack of stovepipe sections, leftover insulation, and bat poop. Ugh!

She asked her father if he had seen the cat anywhere, and he had not.

"You know, honey, he's an old tomcat, and he's probably just taken a trip to meet a lady."

She knew that made sense. Before all their kitties had been fixed a tom from somewhere away would come, hang around for a few days, and disappear, back to wherever his home was. She knew that. He'd be back. She knew he'd be back.

Several days passed, then a week. Her hopes of ever seeing the big Cat again sank lower with each visit to the barn.

What she didn't know, was that Puffer had *already* found Cat!

The day after he had struggled back to the barn, Thumbs and Puffer went on one of their leisurely mousing expeditions. The sun had melted all the snow that covered the stone wall between the barn and the house, and they went there first. Each cat draped itself over a warm stone of appropriate size and shape, and watched. Well . . . they watched the ground around the base of the wall for a little while, but before long their eyes drooped, and they each took a comfortable snooze.

When they awoke, they climbed down and walked to the big stone platform alongside the barn. The two cats investigated each niche and crevice between the rocks, looking for a telltale tip of mouse tail or whisker. The only thing Puffer found was one of the crisp, translucent skins that Ribbon snake had shed the previous summer. Thumbs drew a blank.

They entered the crawl space beneath the barn. Thumbs turned to the right, and walked down the slope toward the stacks of used lumber and chicken wire rolls. Mouse often used the maze between the boards to travel between his nest in the north foundation wall to the southeast corner of the cellar. There, outside the supporting mass of rock, grew a vine of Concord grapes. They fell to the ground in late October—treasures for Mouse. Thumbs knew that. Thumbs knew a lot more about Mouse than Mouse would have wished.

Puffer went straight ahead, and lay down on the bone-dry dirt in the middle of the space. From there she could see down through the storage area where Thumbs had gone, and to the left she could see the tight places where the beams supporting the floor above almost touched the ground.

She could hear Rooster searching for bits of grain in the cracks between the floorboards under Horse's bucket. Horse was not a tidy eater.

The horses and sheep had been let out for the day, and once Rooster gave up and went outside to search for barnyard fare, the building was silent.

She heard Crow calling, faintly. He was far beyond the birches. Beyond the spruce woods, too. He was in the marsh, trying to assemble his kin to council. Maybe in their travels they would find Owl today. If they did, every crow within miles would come to scold and harass until he flew off to a more protected place.

The silence around her was quite complete. The powdery dirt on the ground absorbed reflected sound. Any squeak or rustle of feet could be traced to its source with

100

the flick of an ear. She heard Thumbs shift his weight when he brushed aside a tiny stone, and she heard three mice scurrying beneath the feed room floor. That floor was too close to the ground for cats to squeeze in. Mouse knew that.

Puffer listened to them anyway. Who knows . . . maybe one of them would come her way.

Then she heard a larger sound: the dry rustle of hay. To her left. Toward the feed room floor. Her eyes narrowed, and she tensed for a spring at whatever might appear from under the beam.

Nothing did.

She waited, not relaxing a bit. But nothing moved.

Something had made that noise!

Puffer crept slowly up the sloping dirt toward the feed room floor. She ducked under a beam, intending to continue on, and under the next. As she stretched her leg forward to take her first step, something made her look to the right.

The space between the beams was a tunnel of shadows, and she strained to see to the foundation wall. At the end was the darkest shadow of all. Cat! He lay curled in the hollow of hay that had comforted him their first night in from the winter woods.

Puffer crept cautiously to his side. He did not stir. She nosed his head carefully, trying to puzzle out the fisher smell. She had no experience with such a smell as this. She did not like it at all, at all. She spoke, quietly . . . "*Rrrrawr.*"

Cat awoke, and stared at her through feverish eyes. He did not have the energy to reply.

She did not understand. She rubbed her face against his jowl, trying to promote another response. There was none. His breathing was raspy, and had a shallow sound. She tried everything she could to entice him to move, even bit his ear softly, several times.

Nothing.

Puffer was confused. She had never seen a sick cat before. Not *this* sick, anyway. What she did not know, was that any animal in the condition Cat was in, usually crawled away and found a secret place to die. Alone.

Thumbs had heard her voice. He abandoned his half-hearted hunt and walked up the grade to the more restricted part of the crawl space.

He didn't like it there. He found it hard to maneuver in the tight spaces without becoming draped with dusty cobwebs. He did not like cobwebs at all. The smaller cats didn't mind. They came mousing up here all the time.

He squeezed beneath the last beam and walked down the flat tunnel and crouched beside Puffer. The two studied Cat for several minutes. They watched his chest as he breathed, for the slight movement it made was the only indication that he was alive. Thumbs could smell the wounds in the big cat's neck. They had begun to fester, and as thick as his neck was, there was an indication that it had begun to swell. Thumbs sniffed the torn foot. It was devoid of the putrid smell of infection, but was heavily crusted with dried blood and all manner of dirt and debris. He settled himself, and began to gently lick the foot. Bit by bit, tiny flecks of moistened crust were removed by his raspy tongue.

Puffer started on the other end.

She concentrated on the big cat's face. Her efforts were less medicinal, more directed toward comfort and moral support.

The various attentions he was receiving roused Cat

from his stupor and he acknowledged them with an instinctive, two syllable *"Urr-urrr."*

During the next few days Puffer and Thumbs went beneath the barn often. Cat was comforted by their attentions, and each time they left him he felt more and more alone. His level of awareness remained about the same. He recognized the sounds of their approach, could visually make out the difference between the two cats, but waves of heat and blurred vision swept over him at regular intervals, obscuring any sense of reality he might have had. He was no longer plagued by direct pain, but was tormented by severe aches that infiltrated every muscle and joint.

One afternoon, Puffer brought him an offering: a mouse. She laid it directly in front of his nose. In ordinary circumstances Cat would have all but swallowed it whole, but now he was far beyond hunger and had no desire for food. He opened his eyes slightly when she set it down, but closed them again, drifting back into his fevered sleep.

Each day that passed the big cat weakened noticeably. He lay on his side now, unable to move anything except the tip of his tail.

One morning several of the other cats followed Puffer below the barn, curious about her attentions there. They lined up side by side in between the two beams, closing off what little light filtered through to the foundation wall.

Cat woke briefly, and when he looked their way he could not see his cat friends at all, only dark shapes, hovering, threatening.

And he was afraid.

Puffer spent most of her time with the dying Cat. She

went upstairs to the food bowls to sustain herself, but spent no time in the loft just lying about or going with Thumbs on a leisurely hunt. She was often not there when feeding time came, and missed the touch of Tracy's hand. The days passed. Puffer kept her vigil deep beneath the barn, cleaning and caring for her giant, wild Cat.

Chapter Ten

Tracy was beginning to give up hope of ever seeing Cat again. It had been two weeks since she had seen him in the barn, and surely if this was home to him now he would have returned by now.

Each time she came to the barn to feed she glanced hopefully into the sheep pen, then climbed to the loft and looked in the various hiding places she knew cats liked. It got more depressing each time she failed to find him, and with every successive visit her efforts dwindled some. She had so looked forward to fulfilling some of her fantasies about him, especially the one she had most often: seeing him curled up at the foot of her bed! That was her favorite. Her disappointment turned to anger sometimes, and she blamed the cat for raising her hopes too high, only to let them be dashed in the end. A little while after something like that would enter her head, Tracy would feel a little guilty, even selfish.

She did notice a change in Puffer's behavior. The kitty would eat some of the kibbles Tracy offered, and promptly disappear. Often Tracy came to the barn and

Puffer was nowhere to be found, even at night. She knew the cat had only ever stayed out all night once. At least she *thought* she knew.

It had been a long time since Puffer had acted this way, Tracy thought. Long time. Not since the last time she'd had . . .

"Kittens, kittens, kittens! Puffer's going to have kittens!" she cried, dashing from the barn toward the house.

Halfway there she brought herself up short—*Wait a minute*. She thought. *Puffer's been fixed!*

"Rats!" The excitement drained from her so fast she got butterflies in her stomach.

Tracy went back to the barn to think. She sat on the stairs surrounded by cats, and when Thumbs came through the front doors she asked, "Thumbs! Where's Puffer?"

He just walked over to her slowly, rubbed himself against her legs, and purred heartily.

That night, Puffer did not appear at feeding time. Now that Tracy was paying attention to the cat's habits she began to worry that maybe Puffer was going out to the woods on hunting trips. She knew that could only last so long. Once Owl or Fisher realized there was a barn cat roaming their territory Puffer would not last long at all. Maybe not even till tomorrow. That thought gave Tracy goose bumps!

She waited for a while, sitting with the cats on the bottom step of the loft stairs. Thumbs sat in her lap, and the others crowded around above and below her, each searching out its own little relationship with a cuff, the back of her coat, even the toe of her boot.

Tracy sat there for over an hour, worrying about

Puffer, and thinking about the big black cat she had so desperately wanted to have for herself. Puffer and Thumbs were as close as barn cats ever get to becoming real pets. But she had always wanted a cat of her very own. A house cat she could cuddle. A cat that would wake her up with a rumbling purr. One that considered Tracy its whole world, and lived in her room.

She sneaked Puffer to her room one night the previous summer, just to try it out. Everything was as she had imagined it might be: the warmth, the gentle rubs and comforting purrs were all there. She had a little trouble getting to sleep, but she didn't care. It was wonderful.

During the night Tracy woke a few times when light sounds invaded her sleep, but drifted off quickly when the cat jumped to the bed and snuggled against her arm.

When she woke, Puffer was there, a pile of gray innocent warmth asleep by her feet. Tracy sat up, reached for the cat, and glanced at her Teddy who sat on the floor right by the bed.

He wasn't sitting.

He was on his back, and one button eye hung down on his cheek, attached by only one thread. She looked around the room. A curtain was torn. Just a bit. A sock found its way from her shoe to the door and all her pencils were spread on the floor.

Tracy's first thought was to clean up the mess and sneak Puffer back to the barn unseen. She was most upset by Teddy's eye, but she had to hurry and get Puffer out. The cat watched, purring her satisfaction at a night well spent.

Tracy didn't forget that night. Her memory tended to gray out the mess, and concentrated on the more important cuddles and purrs.

She wondered if a barn cat could ever live in a house. If one could, maybe a wild black marsh cat could do it, too.

Tracy was returned from her dreamy state by the sound of a voice.

"Tracy . . . Tracy honey . . . Homework!"

Ugh! Yuck.

Two days later, Saturday arrived. Saturday, Saturday . . . no school! When Tracy fed, Puffer was there and ate breakfast with the rest of the cats. The girl noticed cobwebs stuck to her tail, and was determined to find where she was spending her time.

The barn was closed tight except for the big doors. The cat *had* to go through the big doors. Had to. Before Puffer finished her meal, Tracy left the barn and hid in the back of one of the trucks. From there she could see anything that came through the doors.

She waited. And waited.

Puffer had finished eating, and now she sat at the top of the stairs washing her paws, and her ears, and her tail, and Thumbs . . . then started in on her paws again.

Tracy wished she had brought a book or something. The monotony was broken by a broad-winged hawk who soared over the barn and flapped out of sight. She wondered what it would be like to have a set of wings—but then, if you had wings, you would probably have to eat snakes and things. Yuck!

Puffer finally appeared and stood in the door. She looked to the right, then looked to the left. Then stepped daintily down to the gravel drive.

Tracy got ready to sneak out of the truck, but then the cat sat down; and washed her paw.

Her left one.

Then she did her right one, too.

Twice.

The girl was about to lose her resolve, when the cat rose, and walked slowly, agonizingly slowly, along the front of the barn, toward the house. As soon as she turned the corner and was out of sight, Tracy jumped from the truck and ran on tiptoe to the barn and peeked around the corner.

A gray tail was disappearing through a gap in the foundation wall. She ran to that point, and on hands and knees peered into the crawl space where the cat had gone. In the dim light she could just make out Puffer's shape moving up the slope to the left, then she crawled under a beam and was lost from sight.

Yuck, and double-yuck. Tracy didn't want to squeeze in there! But she knew she could. She had done it once, playing hide-and-seek, and almost got stuck.

She was determined to see why Puffer went there, so she backed out of the hole and went to the house for an electric lantern. And a banana.

Tracy told her dad what she was about to do. She always did. He insisted on knowing every adventure's path and about how long she'd be gone, so if she didn't appear he could follow her route and be sure to find her somewhere along the way.

"All right, honey, but be careful," he said. "Look out for the family of four-foot spiders!"

"Hey, Daddy, cut that out!"

"Okay, honey, just take 'er easy."

She slipped out the door. She really didn't want to hear any more about four-foot-long spiders, even if she did know there was no such thing. But she thought about it on the way to the barn. Yuck, yuckitty-yuck!

Tracy entered the crawl space on her hands and knees, and headed toward the spot where Puffer had crept under the beam. She could see it would be hard to squeeze under at that point, so she moved over to the left, where the ground fell away a bit toward the south wall. There was more headroom there. She went beneath the beam, then turned to her right and crawled between that one and its neighbor to the north. The ground rose as she inched along, and she had to push the light ahead of her as headroom grew tight. She pretended she was exploring an unmapped cave, searching for a pirate's treasure of gold. Where was Puffer?

At about the middle of the barn, the ground leveled off. The beams on either side of her were hand-hewn twelve-by-twelves, and they reached almost to the dirt. Tracy was on her stomach now, dragging herself along with her forearms and elbows, and pushing hard with the toes of her boots. Once she realized she was on level ground, she set the lantern on the dirt and flipped its switch.

The wooden tunnel flooded with light.

There, sitting on a pile of hay not ten feet in front of her, sat Puffer.

"Puffer! You silly kitty, what are you doing down here?" The glare from the lantern made the cat turn away.

At first Tracy thought Puffer came here to get away from it all.

Then, over the top edge of the hay she saw a furry black line stretching almost from beam to beam. At first she was frightened. Her heart did a flip, and flying butterflies filled her chest. She thought of hairy black spiders, four feet long!

*   *   *

110

"*Rowrrr*" . . . Puffer's voice was a welcome sound. Tracy reached her hand out and the old cat started to purr, and rubbed her cheek against the tips of the outstretched glove.

The girl inched forward, her heart still pounding at the sight of black fur. She pushed the lantern up onto the hay.

"Cat! Oh, Puffer . . . it's Cat! Oh, Puffer! Puffer! Puffer!"

The gray cat turned and looked at the huge black form lying in the hay.

Tracy took off her glove, put her hand on Cat, and withdrew it sharply. All she felt was fur and bones! At first she was repulsed by its uncatlike feel . . . almost as though it were dead! Then the beam of light picked up a movement of hair, and she could tell he was breathing still. He smelled very bad, but she didn't care. He was alive, and he was hers.

The girl's first thought was to get her dad, but she knew he couldn't fit here, beneath the floor.

What to do, what to do. She wished there was room to turn around.

She thought of dragging Cat out by a leg. But she decided he might come apart! Drag . . . drag, of *course* drag! She left the light where it sat and scootched herself backward as fast as she could. Where the ground dropped away and she could sit up a bit, she ripped off her coat, then crawled back up the tunnel to where the sick cat lay.

Tracy spread her coat on the ground as flat as she could, then lay over on her side and reached for Cat. He coughed sharply as she grabbed each hind leg, and it scared her half to death! But she didn't lose her hold.

111

As gently as she could, Tracy pulled the cat over her coat till he was lying fully upon it. Puffer got on, too, but she got shooed off. One cat to pull was quite enough!

The big cat was dimly aware of lights, a voice, and pressure on his legs, but was too far gone to even care.

Tracy labored backward a few inches at a time, then pulled the corner of her jacket as hard as she could, dragging Cat closer to light, and perhaps even life. She knew that he was in desperate shape. She dragged and she sweat and she wished out loud, "Don't let him die . . . don't let him die . . . don't let him. Don't let him . . . don't *let* him!"

She dragged him to where she could almost stand up, looked at Puffer sitting next to the wasted shell of Cat . . . and ran from the barn.

"Daddy! Daddy, Daddy! Come quick, Daddy!"

Chapter Eleven

Cat was aware of very little that happened to him during the next two days. Every so often he would regain consciousness when he, or a part of him was moved. Usually his eyes did not open, and when they did, only vague, gray shapes filtered through.

On the third day, a tube connected to a vein in his leg was removed, and he got shots of electrolytes beneath his skin, to help build up his dehydrated form. The morning of the fifth day dawned. Cat opened his eyes, and for the first time, his focus was clear. He was still too weak to change his position, but he could see.

Bars.

He had never seen such things before, nor had he ever been in a small stainless steel box. In a way it was quite like being reborn, for nothing familiar met his eye. He did not relate to the newspapers beneath him, and had never seen a blank white wall. The smells were strange, and the sounds he heard gave no clues at all.

Cat slept on and off all that day. At one point he noticed his bandaged foot. It no longer hurt, but was a curious sight, and Cat tried to move it for a closer look. He couldn't. Well, he *moved* it, but couldn't raise it up to his face at all. A wide plastic disc was secured around his neck so he couldn't reach any part of himself with his teeth, to chew. He didn't like that at all. And he didn't like bars.

Later that day Cat awoke and heard voices close by. He was able to raise up on his elbows now, and pressed his cheek hard against the bars in the door of the cage. To the right was a wall lined with cages like his. His heart jumped. Each one held a cat! Well, not *every* one. On the bottom row, in a cage by the wall sat a baby beaver, gnawing contentedly on a willow shoot!

Big cats, small cats, in colors of all kinds. Some were lying down, some were very sick, but a few peered hopefully through their bars, waiting for someone familiar to appear through the door.

Cat was still weak, but in his excitement called out, *"RAAhhowwrrrrrr!"*

The other cats froze. Shocked. One cringed against the back of his cage. Behind other bars, a fluffy white kitten moved her head from side to side, wide-eyed, trying to see what had made the awful noise.

Beaver paid no attention. She just gnawed.

Cat waited for some response. Anything. But there were no sounds other than the contented scrapes of beaver teeth.

It was a puzzle for Cat to see the beaver here. There was no water. No marsh or dam. No ferns grew along the edge of white tiles. There was no sunlight, no dancing shadows, no sweet smell of spruce wood or pine. No wind.

And crows . . . the big cat had never been so far re-

114

moved that he didn't hear the animated voice of Crow, even in the barn. A beaver in a shiny box: a puzzle for Cat, and probably a big one for Beaver, too!

The sound Cat made had reached every ear in every room of the building.

Evening office hours were in full swing. The waiting room was full of pets and their humans, all of whom rolled their eyes when they heard Cat's voice. The veterinarian heard it, too. She had just spent exasperating time listening to a silly woman relate details of her toy poodle's birthday party, and was now patiently cleaning mites from an aging basset's smelly ear. All the while she had been thinking how much nicer it would be to be sitting by a pond with a baby beaver.

When her thoughts were shattered by the voice of Cat, the vet handed her assistant the swab she was using on the old dog's ear, and left the room. As she passed the waiting room there were questions in the eyes of those assembled there. . . .

"It's a cat. Just a cat," she said. "Big!" And she held her hands apart to show Cat's size. Everyone looked at each other as she passed from view. They thought she was kidding.

"Hey, Beave!" She said, as she hurried into the cage room. "Hello, cats, cats, cats, cats!"

She approached the cage that held Cat a bit more slowly. "Hey, big cat. How you tonight? Hi, kitty. Boy, you sure are some old *big*!"

Cat was still propped up on his elbows. If he had been stronger he would have gotten up and pressed himself into the farthest corner of the steel box. No matter how used to Tracy he had become, Cat still harbored great mistrust for anything that walked on two legs. The vet came close enough to rest the back of her hand against the bars, only inches in front of the big cat's face. He became as tense as his wasted body would allow, and from deep within his chest uttered a low, lingering growl.

"Oh, kitty-cat, come on now, come on now, kitty. Be a good kitty."

She unlatched the door carefully, and inched it open just enough to slide her hand inside the cage. She held it in front of, and slightly lower than his head. Cat leaned forward an inch and sniffed in the direction of the offered hand. Again, he repeated the ominous growl.

"Cat, you're an old poop!" At this she removed her hand and latched the door. "Sounds to me like you're strong enough to go home."

A few minutes later the vet returned with a small dish containing some lumpy, mushy stuff, and she carefully placed it inside the cage. To Cat it looked like lumpy, mushy stuff, but it smelled interesting. He waited until she had left the room before he tested the mess with the tip of his tongue. It tasted *better* than just interesting! The first solid food to pass his lips in several weeks. It disappeared with astonishing speed.

Good. Much better than dry kibbles. Maybe not as good as Grouse, but good.

Though he had no idea where he was or how he got there, a gentle hand had offered food, and he did not feel threatened. Cat slept well that night, and dreamed of hay, warm, kinky lambs, and a girl.

He heard her voice when she whispered, "Oh, Cat. I love you, Cat. Cat kitty, we're going to take you home now, Cat."

He opened his eyes slowly and Tracy was still in front

of him, appearing as an extension to his dream. "Home, Cat, we're going home," she repeated.

When he looked past her and saw the Daddy, the veterinarian and two assistants staring his way, he tensed, and again the low growl came from deep within him. Too many eyes. Too many eyes.

Tracy turned to the group and said, "Ple-e-ease let me do it. I can do it. Really I can. You know I can, Daddy."

He nodded. "I guess you're right, honey, you give it a try. Just be careful." And with that, he and the others left the room.

Tracy and her father had brought along a large dog traveling case for the big cat to ride home in. He couldn't fit in the cardboard carriers the vet supplied for normal-size cats. She lifted it with some difficulty and put it on the floor in front of Cat's cage, and opened the door.

"Oh, Cat. You are my beautiful, wild cat." She slowly opened the door to his cage and slipped her arm inside. "You are so thin, Cat. You'll eat more now. I'll feed you milk and meat and vitamins galore, and we'll make you shine again, like you did before." She smiled. "See, old Cat, you've made me into a poet, now."

Cat felt soothed by the familiar voice, and he lowered his lids as her gentle fingers felt their way along his sides. When he opened them again she was half-inside the cage, reaching both hands along his sides, down his legs and back again, over his ears and along his neck, "Oh, Cat, you are *really* mine now, I just *know* you are."

The giant cat began to purr, quietly at first, then the volume increased till the steel walls around him thrummed, projecting his pleasure throughout the room.

117

The little white kitten watched intently, then began to purr in her own baby way.

Tracy braced her knees against the floor, and lifted Cat gently out of the door. His purr did not falter as she struggled to arrange him comfortably in the case they had brought. Her winter barn coat cushioned him there, and he could smell Puffer and Thumbs, and old banana peel, too!

Chapter Twelve

During the next few weeks, Tracy was able to spend a great deal of time caring for Cat. Spring vacation started just three days after he had been brought back to the barn, and it was rare that the girl could be found anywhere but with him.

At first, she kept him in a large, airy cage made of rectangular turkey wire. She put it up in the loft and spread hay over the bottom, enough so that Cat could have himself a deep nest similar to the ones the other cats molded for themselves. A little like a chicken nest, really.

Her reasoning for the cage (with a little advice from her father), was that it would keep the other animals away from him till he was strong enough to put up with their attentions, and also, it would prevent him from hurting himself in any way.

Cat didn't mind.

He didn't mind the warm mixture of milk and canned cat food Tracy brought to him four times a day. He didn't mind the comforting feel of her hand as she massaged the long muscles that ran the length of his back, and he certainly didn't mind the sound of her voice as she lay on her back by his cage, talking about the fun they would have when he could be up and about, sharing adventures of all kinds. He didn't mind. The girl fast became his world. Once awake in the early hours his eyes never left the space between the two barn doors till she appeared.

Tracy had all kinds of creative visions concerning Cat. Mostly adventurous ones. But what she liked most to think about was all the time they would spend in the woods together when he got well. She had always been a bit nervous when she went into the woods alone before, but now, now with giant Cat at her side her horizons had no limit. Cat grew and grew in her mind sometimes until she could see herself riding him, searching the woods for a great wild boar with no more of a weapon in her hands than a pink lasso! Together they raced across the arctic wastes on a mission to bottle the northern lights. They would be heroes. No one would ever have to change a light bulb again!

Cat grew stronger, very fast. Once he began to fill out a bit the cage was put away, and he was able to move about the barn at will. His body began to tone, and though he was missing some of his toes he didn't seem to be much handicapped by the loss. Once school was back in session he spent many hours moving throughout the barn, exercising, building muscle, and learning the finer points of climbing with only thirteen toes.

Tracy spent as much time with Cat as homework would allow. On weekends they would go outside the barn with Thumbs and Puffer and go for walks. The fluffy, gray cat never went too far, but Thumbs did. Sometimes he would be the guide and lead them all the way through the birch woods to the big mossy rock where Puffer and Cat first met.

The first time they went there, Cat investigated the hollow log. He went inside for a moment, turned himself around and lay down in the opening. Tracy and Thumbs sat side by side on a thick bed of lichens just a few feet away.

A gentle breeze swayed a single strand of long-abandoned cobweb in front of Cat's eyes. He watched it with a detached expression. He watched it, but not really. His eyes were upon it, but his mind was filled with the smell of the rotted log and a memory of deep snow and a bellyful of snowshoe hare.

Some evenings, after Tracy had left the barn, Cat lay in the loft listening to peeper frogs singing. He remembered that song from his earlier days. His memories then wandered to Frog, and moist cool shadows beneath a forest of ferns, then on to the beaver dam, and minnows, sparkling in the sun.

Tracy had hoped the big cat would be just like Puffer and Thumbs: that she would be his whole world. The two barn cats seemed to exist for her only, spending their days in limbo, just waiting for her to appear with food, caresses, and gentle talk. Their attention was focused only upon *her*, whenever she was around.

Cat, on the other hand, no matter how receptive he was to her attentions, sometimes had a distracted look. She compared it to the times company came and talked about things that didn't interest her much. Often she would listen, to be polite, but her mind was in the barn, or in the woods somewhere.

That was it. Perhaps Cat was being polite. . . .

He cared for the girl, he enjoyed the company of the

other cats and the comforts the hayloft had to offer, but when he heard Crow chortling in the pines or the distant call of Loon, something inside Cat became unsettled. He had no logical way of comparing thoughts, no facts tumbling through his mind, just a feeling.

The days they would wander were the best times for Cat. He felt cleaner, freer somehow. The air was clean and fresh, and the webs that Spider made glistened in the early morning light. The ones in the barn were dull with dust, and were mostly spun in dark, musty places beyond the reach of sun.

Tracy noticed the big cat seemed more animated when they went on walks. His golden eyes were rarely still. He never failed to notice the movement of a leaf or the fleeting shadow of a bird that flew overhead, and his ears were constantly alert for the slightest sound.

Toward the middle of June they walked to the field across the road to see if blossoms had formed on the blueberries yet. Tracy's father had spread lime on the land years before, trying to sweeten the soil so he could get hay to grow. But it didn't work very well. Here and there the acid-loving blueberry plants clung to life in ever-widening patches. They were Tracy's favorite.

She and Cat investigated around slabs of granite ledge that thrust above the ground, and found enough blossoms to guarantee an early August feast of blueberry muffins, and pancakes, too.

Then they walked toward the pond that nestled low in a basin toward the middle of the field, out of sight of the road. This was one of Tracy's favorite spots. There was a very large rock at the edge of the pond, and she often climbed it and sat on top. She had a good view of the field from there, and could see herons stalking the water's edge for frogs, and sometimes deer, and sunsets. This time water striders were the only things that moved, and the tops of waving grass. And Cat.

When the girl had climbed the rock, he had gone down to the water's edge to take a drink.

From the corner of his eye he saw a movement! Ever so slight.

Tracy could see him clearly, just to the left of her rock. He was in a half-crouch, his head turned slightly to the right, and not a hair moved. For a moment she watched, fascinated. She had never seen him hunt before.

With no warning at all, Cat sprang beneath the rock, out of her sight. He moved so quickly it shocked her some, for he moved his whole body as fast as most cats just flick a paw!

She flopped on her belly and eased herself slowly over the edge of the rock to see, and down below Cat was enjoying a meal of frog.

"Yuck, and *double-yuck*!" she said.

When he finished his meal, Cat jumped to the top of the rock, carefully licked the water from his fur, and tidied up his paws. Tracy had no way of knowing, but for many nights Cat had supplemented his barn dish fare with dessert of frog.

When he finished grooming, Tracy climbed down off the rock and headed through the tall timothy grass, up-hill, toward home. Halfway to the road she turned. Cat was not there. She looked back down her path toward the rock and saw he was still sitting there, looking out across the pond.

"Hey, Cat! Here kitty, kitty, kitty!"

At first he did not move. He just stared across the pond and into the pine woods that grew beyond.

"Here, kitty, kitty . . . Hey, Cat, c'mon!"

He reluctantly jumped from the rock, and next appeared trotting through the tunnel of disturbed grasses toward the waiting girl.

He did not touch his meal that night.

Since he had regained his health Cat had been reduced to eating the same old dry kibbles the rest of the cats ate. Sometimes Tracy would sneak a meaty leftover from a dinner plate out to the barn for a treat. He looked forward to those times. What the girl did *not* know was that Cat went on regular hunting trips now. Sometimes to the woods, sometimes to the pond, always at night after the barn was asleep he left more domestic souls behind. He roamed free and clear, prowling the land as he was born to do. Slowly, old One-Eye's giant son was becoming part of the woods again.

Tracy's father could see it coming. Though he had no personal relationship with Cat, he could see from a distance the animal's attitude begin to change.

Tracy did, too, but she didn't want to acknowledge it. She could still pet the cat and he reacted with all the fervor of previous months, to a point where she still called him hers. But she could easily see he was not as dependent on her now, and it hurt her through.

"Honey," her father said one night when he was trying hard to explain about Cat without breaking her heart, "Honey, that big old cat isn't really quite like the rest of 'em you know. You can just *look* at him and tell that, though, can't you? But it's more than just what he looks like. He may love you a lot. Actually, I'm sure he does."

Tracy didn't think she was going to like what he was

about to say, and a lump started to well up in her throat.

He continued, "You know, you are probably the only person he's *ever* cared for, and that's something special you'll remember for the rest of your life. You've seen how he looks when you're out in the woods . . . sorta lookin' faraway, like he's got his mind on something else? Well, he does, honey, he does."

Here it comes, she thought. *Here it comes.*

"He's special, honey. In his great big heart he's special, and that same heart is as wild as any that ever pumped life through a bobcat or lynx.

"Now, you're real special, too. There's something different about you. Something that lets animals *trust.* I dunno what it is, but you've always had it. Now, because of that, I know you understand 'em more than most of us do, and even though you don't want to admit it, you know what's best for 'em. What's best for Cat."

She knew. She had seen the faraway look in those golden eyes many times during the past few weeks. She could just imagine Cat barreling through deep snow in pursuit of Hare, or prowling along the marsh's edge, searching for Frog. She imagined him sleeping in a hollow log during a sun-drenched August day. Shadows of ferns cooled him there, and a mattress of rotted wood and moss provided a soft cushion on which to lie.

"Oh, Daddy . . . I know," she whispered. Then, after a long silence, in a voice he could barely hear, "But, Daddy, I . . . I do love him so."

"I know y'do, honey. I know y'do." He wrapped her in his arms and whispered . . .

"I know y'do."

When Tracy went to the barn the following morning, the giant cat was gone.

126

Epilogue

The summer passed all too fast to suit Tracy. Blueberry time came and went, there were a few trips to the beach, some fishing with her dad on Duck Puddle, and finally, in late August, a night at the Union Fair. She ate too much cotton candy, and he ate *way* too many pepper and sausage sandwiches. They both had aching stomachs the following day!

The only solution, of course, was a brisk paddle up the creek, to Duck Puddle. Of course, of course! With fishing rods. Tracy never went near a likely piece of water without a fishing rod in her hand.

Once they entered the pond they paddled eastward, toward the outlet of Beaver Brook. There were shallows there, and lily pads. Now and again they had caught a big bass who had been waiting in the shadows beneath the cover of pads, waiting for someone smaller to swim from the mouth of the brook!

"Daddy, could we go up and see the dam?"

"Sure, honey. Why not."

Her father did the paddling here. He proceeded slowly,

127

because Tracy liked to look down into the shallow water. Sometimes she saw fish, sometimes turtles, as they flailed their little legs in a frantic effort to get out of sight.

The brook was very narrow, and everyone they passed had to swim under the canoe to get away. It was as good as looking at a glass aquarium!

Grasses drooped over each side of the canoe as they slipped silently up the slow-moving stream, and the ribbon of water narrowed till it seemed as though they were moving through a tunnel of grass.

"S-s-s-t . . .*S-s-s-s-s-st*."

Tracy barely heard her father's hiss. She turned slowly toward him. He motioned ahead of the canoe with the blade of his paddle and placed a finger over his lips.

She nodded, and as slowly as she could, turned around again to face the front.

They had just drifted around the last bend below the beaver dam. . . .

Cat!

Fifty yards ahead, the great black shape glided slowly along the top of the dam.

It was all she could do to remain silent.

Cat reached the center, where water trickled over the top of the dam and flowed into the brook. He lay down, to watch minnows flash and Beaver toil, and maybe even watch the sun go down.

"Oh, Cat," Tracy whispered to herself. "Oh, Cat. You really are my Cat, you know."